Bred by the WOLFMAN

LYONNE RILEY

introduction

Dee is tired of working minimum wage jobs, so she takes a position at DreamTogether, where she'll anonymously carry a monster's baby in exchange for a sizable salary. But when her first client, "Bill" the wolfman, shows her the time of her life, Dee will be changed forever.

Russ has always wanted a cub of his own, but he's exhausted all possible options except one: hiring an anonymous surrogate at DreamTogether. While he expects a perfunctory visit breeding a human, he discovers an incredible and delectable woman—and his instincts recognize her as his mate.

But after parting ways, neither of them knows the other besides a fake name. Can Russ find out Dee's true identity, and convince her that they should raise their cub together?

CONTENT WARNINGS

May contain spoilers.

- Breeding

- Anonymous sex
- Knotting
- Surrogacy
- Pregnancy
- Stalking
- Cheating (FMC cheats on other man with MMC)
- Dog attack
- Marking (with a bite, non-consensual)
- FMC slaps MMC
- Hunting and eating of wild animals
- Birth
- Birth complications (brief)
- Premature baby
- More breeding

To my #1 hype girl

one

DEE

IT WAS one thing to sign up for this. It's a very different thing to actually be strapped in, face down, my feet in steel stirrups with padded bands anchoring me to the bench. The stirrups hold me so my legs are wide open and I'm fully exposed, my ass up to the sky and the gentle air conditioning brushing over my most sensitive parts.

We're not supposed to look at them, and they're not supposed to look at us. Those are the rules, or so I was told. It was also in the documentation DreamTogether gave me, which I was instructed to closely review before my first day.

It seemed like a great idea when I scribbled my name on the dotted line and dated three sheets of carbon-copy paper. Good pay for nine months of work and three months of recovery time, mostly work-from-home? Not to mention the excellent health insurance, which I've desperately needed—the best money can buy, no surprise. This is a spendy opera-tion, and the monsters that come in here are either wealthy already, or have scratched and saved their pennies for many years to make their dream a reality.

I wonder which kind of monster I'll get. As nervous as I feel right now, I'll take any of them, as long as I don't have to wear a visor and work late nights over a hot fryer.

I was given a month to prep after signing the contract. During my prep period, DreamTogether gave me a device to help spread me for my first appointment, called a "dilator." Every night I set it just a little wider, then lay back on my bed, covered the silicone exterior in lube, and worked it into my vagina. Monsters are big, much more than humans, and for my own comfort I needed to be prepared. Responsibly I used it every night, setting it wider and wider, until I could take a girth that surprised even me.

I could probably get into fisting.

Now I'm in my probationary period, and how well I do during this first pregnancy will tell the company whether I can do more in the future. Of course I want to do more, and see if I can save up a nice nest egg for when I reach my five-pregnancy limit.

This job is perfect, really. I can spend my time doing things I enjoy, and not worry about trying to scrounge up a living. There are so many hobbies I've wanted to try, but I'm too busy working at McFlips to do anything but veg in front of the TV and go to bed in my off-hours. Now all my needs will be met by the stipend I'm given, and I can finally get my wisdom teeth removed.

But with my clothed chest pressed against the bench and padded, leather ties strapped around my arms, I'm not so sure it was my best move ever. My heart starts beating faster as I try to adjust myself, but the straps keep me held down. I know it's all for my own safety, but left alone in the silence like this, I'm sweating, and I wonder if I've made a huge mistake.

The room is sterile, disturbingly so. The walls are painted white and the floor is white tile. It all smells like it was recently cleaned. The bench is steel, and it makes me wonder how wild some monsters get when they're mating. My bench is heavily padded to keep me safe from claws and hooves and whatever else, and DreamTogether assured me that there are cameras watching and listening at all times, in case a monster gets out of control. Then, they'll intervene.

And just to make everything easier, a bottle of lube sits on the little table next to me.

I have an appointment at one p.m. on the dot, but I can see the face of my watch from here, and it's 1:05. I've only been in this position for a few minutes and I'm already growing tired of it.

Suddenly, a roar shakes the building. After a few moments there comes another rumbling growl, and I gape at the wall. What on earth was that? One of the other girls had mentioned she was on her third visit with a dragon, who had huge claws that gripped the entire bench. Once, she said, he pulled the whole thing out of the cement when he orgasmed.

I wonder how human-dragon offspring work, and how much of a bitch it would be to carry that particular baby—or whatever dragons call them. I hope she's getting hazard pay.

When I signed up, I was given a list of possible monsters and checked off the ones I was comfortable with. I don't remember everything on it now, but I'd okayed most of them except for the dragon, most notably. I'm glad I did.

But I could get anything. Perhaps a minotaur, or even a cyclops. They're all large creatures, and I'll most likely make good use of the work I've done with the dilator.

I tick off another few minutes, my vagina growing drier by the moment. Damn it, where is he? Why would he be late to such an important appointment?

As if summoned by my thoughts, the door flies open so fast and so hard that it bangs on the wall. I cringe, and a husky voice quickly says, "I'm so sorry." Much more quietly the door is closed, and reflexively I turn my head to try and see who's behind me.

"I thought we weren't supposed to look?" the voice says, deep and male and gravelly.

Blushing, I turn back around. "Right. My bad."

He's here. He's really here, and I'm really doing this. I wrap my hands around the padded grips underneath my chest, because my fingers have started shaking.

It's like I'd told Liesel. I'm excited about this. It's a massive career opportunity and could, potentially, feel really good. I'd tried to date a monster, but for the most part, humans and monsters alike tend to marry within their species. It's easiest that way, when we often live in different cities and different housing developments, and work at different companies. We don't even frequent the same bars, so my chances of meeting someone eligible is generally slim.

But one thing we humans have that monsters don't? High fertility rates, and a wide range of compatibilities. Almost any monster can mate with a human and produce offspring, and so companies like DreamTogether were born.

Heh. Born.

Over my shoulder, I hear a deep inhale of breath. "You're nervous," the low voice says. "I can smell it on you, my dear."

Oh, great. A monster that can *smell* how I feel. The last thing I want is to be giving off the scent of fear while he's trying to get hard.

"Sorry," I say. "First time."

There's another huff behind me, and then I feel soft fur touching my hips. Fur? Maybe a yeti? The dull tips of claws brush over my skin.

"Your first time taking wolfman dick, or just in general?" he asks.

I crack a smile. So he's a wolfman, and a dirty talker. I can do that.

"In general," I say. "You're my first client."

My visitor snorts. "Client," he says with derision. "Is that what I am? Just another client?"

I furrow my brow. How am I supposed to answer that? Of course he is. That's the whole setup here. I'm the provider, he's the client. He's paying me for my services.

"Yes?" I answer tentatively. "I mean, I can't even see your face. This is a transaction, isn't it? You pay. I carry your baby."

"Cub," the apparent wolfman corrects me.

I nod. "Of course. That."

For a moment there's silence, and I wonder if I've fucked something up. But I'm not sure what else he wants from me. His hands haven't moved, though, and wow, they're huge. I wonder what he looks like. Then, as if cued by my imagination, he draws his fingers down toward the swell of my ass.

"Hmm." Claws gently prod my flesh, squeezing me. I wonder if this is part of the process or not. I thought it would be a little more get-in-and-get-out, like a pee test. Instead, my client is testing me out, massaging my butt in a way that is, frankly, pretty erotic.

I hear the wolfman sniff again. "Ah," he hums. "Much better." He pulls the cheeks of my ass apart, exposing me to the air even further. Instead of earlier, though, when no one was here, now I know he's watching, and a shiver runs down from my throat to my groin. I feel myself clench inside as his clawed finger reaches deeper in, spreading me apart, drawing my labia away from my opening. I feel the air conditioner again, even more acutely—and then, hot breath.

"Such a beautiful, hairy pussy," the wolfman says, growling low in his throat.

What? Nobody's ever said anything like that to me. I didn't bother trimming, because I'm not here for the sex. I do have some thick, dark hair that I've always been self-conscious about, but instead I feel a tiny dribble of wet drool land on my leg in the stirrup.

He really likes it that much?

The wolfman keeps me spread with one hand, then trails the other down the inside of my thigh, toward that place where I'm tingling. His claw gently traces my skin, stopping just short of my clit. I thought he'd simply smear himself with lube and get on with it, but that doesn't seem to be the case.

Not that I mind. Though this teasing... it's turning me on a lot more than it should. This is supposed to be business, nothing more.

But it clearly means more to my client. I guess I should go along with it, if that's what he wants.

"You're wet," the wolfman remarks, curling his finger so now his knuckle is stroking my labia. He swoops it down, brushing over the tip of my clit, and I can't help the little gasp that escapes me. I'm rewarded with a chuckle. "Do you like that, little human?"

"Sure," I say. "You found the clitoris. Congratulations."

A guffaw of a laugh fills the room. That knuckle rubs across my clit again, more roughly this time, and I moan. I can't deny it feels good, but I don't like all this teasing.

"You're funny," he says, looping his knuckle around to

repeat the motion. "That will be a good trait for my cub to have."

That is why he's here, after all. He wants a child of his own. I wonder if he has a wife or a mate, and they've been struggling to have a "cub." Or maybe he's single and hasn't been able to start a family, but wants one.

I'm already starting to hope he's the latter kind. I don't want to think about some other wolf-lady he's been fingering this way. I hope he's rich and single, maybe some kind of CEO, and can give our kid a good life.

I can't believe I'm thinking like that already. We don't even know if his sperm will take. It might require quite a few visits, they warned me. They'll schedule one a month, right before ovulation, until I'm pregnant.

And it's not like I know him at all. That's the point—that we don't know each other and have no attachments. But that's hard to keep at the top of my brain when he's gliding back and forth over my clit, making me wetter and wetter with each pass. My pussy flutters, and I hear that deep inhale again behind me.

"There we go," he says. That's all this is. He's just trying to get me ready for him. It isn't a personal thing, meant for my pleasure.

That's when I feel something wet brush over my pussy.

I buck against the bench, overwhelmed instantly by the sensation of it. Is he really *going down* on me? I hear a muffled chuckle.

"Damn," he says, and there comes a slurping noise like he's licking his chops. "That's good. I knew I picked right."

I'm poised to say something about propriety and professionalism when that huge tongue laves over me again, this time down and over my clit. I moan as it circles there, flicking across it with abandon, then travels back to my slit again. My hips respond instinctually as the wolfman presses his tongue inside me, and I'm shocked by the size of it.

How big is this guy?

I can't manage out words as he fucks me with his tongue, then quickly returns to my clit, back and forth. Soon I'm squirming and moaning, my pussy aching for something that isn't there. Again that tongue twists its way into my channel, licking upward and then dragging along the inside of me.

"Oh, fuck," I manage out, my whole body snapping up. He does it again, rubbing against my inner wall, and I can already feel my orgasm coming on. "God, yes." I can't stop the words tumbling out of my mouth.

Again he teases my clit, and again he fills me up, devouring me. I can't help it when I go screeching right over the end of the train tracks, and something opens up inside me, unleashing a torrent of liquid.

"Oh no," I whimper as his tongue rapidly licks me. "I'm so sorry. I don't know what just happened, I—"

"You've never squirted?" the wolfman asks, bafflement in his voice. "It's normal." Then he chuckles to himself, a rather self-satisfied sound. "I'm glad I could be your first one, again."

Claws gently brush over the thick flesh of my ass, where he pulls my cheeks apart once more.

"Will you be done staring soon?" I ask, my pussy wide open and begging to be filled with something—anything.

Another booming laugh. But then his voice drops to a growl as he says, "You want my cock inside you, do you?"

I groan with frustration. I can't believe I'm asking him to do the very thing he *paid good money* to come and do to me. But I'm horny and hungry and his filthy mouth is turning me on.

"Yeah," I snap. "I do. So what are you waiting for?"

There's no laugh this time, but a deep, hungry growl. Then comes a sound like a belt unbuckling, and clothes sliding down fur. Another rustle—maybe he's even taking off his shirt. Getting fully naked in order to have sex with me.

Oh, god. That's what he's going to do now. I'm about to get fucked by a real, live wolfman, so he can put a "cub" in me.

"What's your name?" I ask suddenly, wanting to know at least one thing about the monster whose offspring I'm about to carry.

"We signed—" he begins.

"No, it's okay if it's a fake one," I clarify quickly for the surveillance cameras. "I just need... um, something. To say. You know."

A hum of amusement comes from behind me. "Bill," he says. "Call me Bill."

That's a fucking weird name to pick.

"Please, Bill," I say, raising my hips higher into the air even though it makes the padded straps tighten. I need what only he can give me, and I need it right now. "Come inside me."

I hear a dangerous growl, and this time when the big, meaty hands grab my ass, the claws dig in.

"Oh, I will," Bill the wolfman says. Something soft and wet nudges at my entrance, and those claws spread me wide again, revealing everything. He's breathing so hard I can feel it against my back. That object slides in further, just a tip, but... it's big. Really big. Though it coasts on how slick I am, there's still only so much give.

"Your cunt is dripping for me, isn't it?" Bill says, gripping me tight. I moan when he urges me to widen for him, and he huffs against my back. "And I'm going to fuck the most wonderful cub into it."

two

RUSS

FUCK. Damn.

She feels perfect. So completely, utterly, blissfully perfect, and I've barely gotten the tip of my cock inside her. And holy shit, she's tight, too. I expected her to be small, given that she's human and everything, but her hot, wet pussy is making my balls tighten up, and a shiver runs down my spine. I'm practically vibrating with how badly I already need to come in her.

What I can see of her is beautiful, the ideal shape for carrying my cub. She has broad hips and a narrow waist and ribcage, her breasts hidden under her shirt. I can get a good idea of their size, though, and I know they'll be perfect, too. Her hair is long and dark, and braided to hang down her neck. I wish I could see what her face looks like, but that's against the rules.

Before I'm even halfway sheathed in her tiny, pink pussy, my body is singing for her. She's ideally compatible with me, just like I am with her. It won't take many visits to fill her up with my cub. Which is too bad, that I won't get to breed her more than a few times here. And then afterwards, I'll be kept away from her until my cub is born.

My instincts don't like that, not at all. But I knew that would happen walking into this—and I'm prepared to curb myself to get what I want.

I don't dive into her all at once, because I can tell her body is already stretched to its limit. I'll need to warm her up first, so my cock doesn't hurt her tiny human cunt.

She must have worked hard just for this much of me to fit.

Then I notice the lube that's been sitting nearby all along, which I should have used before I tried this. But I was too starving to be inside her.

I thrust shallowly, just a few times to soak up the warmth of her, the pulsing clench of her. She's whimpering and moaning with every stroke, even though I'm doing very little. She's a sensitive thing, I'll need to remember that. I'm mesmerized by the way her lower lips spread wide for me, those delicate black hairs decorating her in flawless curls.

When I pull out of her, she whines in objection. "Why did you stop?"

I like that I've already turned this mouthy woman into a mess.

"I'll be back," I tell her, then reach for the lube. I slather my paw in it, then slide it all along my length. For good measure, I rub the come dripping out of my tip all over her before I push back inside her delicious pussy.

"Ah!" she cries out, falling forward on the bench. I slide in deeper this time, but not so deep that I hurt her. I need her to open up for me, so I can fit my knot into her.

That's the way to make sure it sticks. I'll fatten her up with my cub, without a doubt.

I glide into her again, my way made even easier by the lube, and more of my cock vanishes inside her. She buckles, and it's good that her legs and feet are strapped in. I squeeze her thighs with my claws as I sink deeper, then pull out, then deeper still. My balls are practically shivering already with the need to fill her.

"Oh, Bill," she says into the face pillow so it muffles her voice. "That's... that's so..."

I lean down, bringing the tip of my snout to her ear. "That's so *what?*"

"Please." Her voice comes out wonderfully desperate. "More, please, Bill."

There we are. Though I really don't love the sound of the name I chose—it was a panic decision.

I give her even more, watching raptly as I'm swallowed up by her. My knot is swelling, the two bulges to either side of my shaft pulsing with the need to release. I reach around her and dig my claws into the bottom of the bench, which is rubber and designed exactly for this. I rub my furry belly across her skin as I yank my cock out, and then thrust into her again, each pump earning a moan or a cry and a soft squeezing from her sweet cunt.

Absolutely flawless. It's taking everything in my power not to let off now.

"Open up for me," I whisper to her, shoving her hair aside with my snout. I plunge deeper with this stroke, so the shallowest end of my knot is starting to push inside her. "Let it all in."

I slow my speed, making each snap of my hips deliberate, reaching farther and farther into her small tunnel. Her cries grow in volume, and she's rapidly nodding her head.

"I'm trying," she moans. "Please. I want it. Give me everything."

She's so wild for me that it's making every inch of my fur tremble, and I'm tearing holes into the rubber on the underside of the bench. My feet scrabble for friction on the tile as I fuck her harder, watching her sweet, stretched pussy open even wider for my knot. She's dripping for me, her pink lips shining under the bright overhead fluorescents as I stroke into her again, and again.

"Take it," I say, burying my nose in her hair to breathe in the smell of her. Oh, fuck, is she perfect, and everything I've always wanted. "Take my knot."

"Yes," she moans as I push even more of it in. There's a wet *slurp* with every thrust, the twin bulges at the base of my cock squeezing almost all the way in before I pull out again, her wetness dripping all over both of us. "More, Bill! More!"

So I obey, and on my next thrust, I manage to shove all of myself inside her. She cries out loudly, collapsing forward on the bench. I have to stand up more now to get the leverage I want, because I'm going to fuck her with my knot until she's screaming.

How I've held back this long, I have no idea.

I slam my whole cock into her, then reel my hips back, only to bury it in her again. Every time she calls out my name, it makes all the hair on my mane and back stand up on end.

How I do wish it was *my* name.

I fuck her even faster, pounding her with my knot, and she starts to tense up all around me. Now I can barely fit inside her, and her walls are clenched so tight I feel like my cock might just pop. She feels better than pure bliss itself.

"Oh, fuck, Bill," she sobs, and my mane is bristling at how sweet and delirious her voice sounds. "Fuck me harder, wolfman, p-please, I'm s-so close..." So I obey, fucking her like my entire life depends on it, clenching my thighs and ass hard so I can slam into her, over and over again.

When she finally comes, it's heavenly. She clamps down tight and wails, her hands clutched like claws around her grips. Her legs go stiff, and suddenly I'm struggling to move at all with how tight she's become.

It's time. I jam my knot inside her as hard as I can, and it slips through her seizing, swollen channel. Then it lodges there, at last.

I moan an agonizing moan as I finally let the dam break and all my come shoots out, more than I think I've ever come before. The bulges of my knot have swollen up fat with blood, and there's no way I'm pulling it out of her anytime soon. The edges of her shining pussy have clamped down around it, nearly strangling my cock.

"Oh," she moans as she suddenly wriggles, and then clenches up again. A mini-orgasm. Her body has taken well to mine already. I stroke her back as the fog of my own climax starts to clear. But I'm still anchored to her, and it will be some time before we can separate.

"How was that, my dear?" I ask, a little sultry. I peel back my lips and lick down from her ear to her neck, and she shivers all over. Her lovely pussy trembles around me.

"Really..." She swallows like her mouth is dry. "Really good." She cranes her neck ever-so-slightly. "Will you come back, Bill?"

"Of course I will," I say, brushing my hand down her spine to her round ass. "I'll see you in one month." I don't know that for sure, but I'm going to hope. I want to know if my hunch about her is right or not—that she might be more to me than some anonymous woman with a great ass, an adorable moan and a pristine pussy.

"Okay. In a month, then." Her shoulders droop. Does that mean she's feeling the attachment, too?

We wait quietly until my knot comes down, and I spend it fantasizing about what she looks like, how she might feel under my hands when she's full of my cub. Not that that will happen. Then, I slowly slide out, cupping my hand under her swollen, puffy cunt to catch the come that sloshes out. She sags against the bench, and I lick each of the cheeks of her butt.

"Thank you," I murmur to her, cleaning her with a towel as best I can. She moans and twitches as I mop her up, and I've never smelled something as beautiful as her covered in my spend.

"Look forward to next time," she says in a sleepy voice, and I wish I could hold her. Instead, I settle for running a claw down her back, then patting her once before leaving the room.

At the reception desk, I'm told that they'll call me before my surrogate is scheduled to ovulate so I can come in for a follow-up appointment. They'll administer weekly tests, but it's likely I'll have to return at least a few times to make sure it sticks. Once it does, they'll let me know, and then I won't have to come in again until my cub is born.

It makes my gut shudder to think I won't be there for her pregnancy. But that's the point of all this: I don't know her, and she doesn't know me. There are penalties for breaking confidentiality, and I could lose my shot at ever having a child of my own if I tried to find out her identity.

When I walk out into the sunshine, though, I feel better

and lighter than I ever have. My body is at peace in a way it's never been before. Mating so thoroughly with such a perfect woman has settled something deep inside me—while a different flame has ignited.

I finally turn my cell phone back on, and it's full of missed calls. Shit. I rush to my car and get in, then slam the door closed. I had taken today off for my appointment, but this is clearly an emergency.

I put on the gas and drive out of the parking lot, though I feel like my mind and my heart are back in that room with the mother of my future cub. She took me so well, and felt so impossibly good around me. Her scent was like nothing else in the world.

Heading away from that building, I'm almost certain that she's my mate.

three

DEE

MY VAGINA IS PRETTY sore after my *experience* with the wolfman. At the same time, I miss it. I wish he could have done it again right after, and then again after that, and then...

I can't get caught up thinking like that. This is a transaction, like I told him. He comes inside me as many times as he can until my test result comes up positive, and then we never see each other again. When the baby is born—his *cub*, as he insists—I'll hand it off to DreamTogether and they'll be reunited with their father.

Then I'll take some time off, and meet the next one.

I doubt, though, that any of my other clients will treat me with such unrestrained desire as the wolfman did. He wanted me, that much was obvious. He wouldn't have lapped at my clit so hungrily if he didn't want to, if all he was after was to get me ready for him.

No, he'd wanted to make me feel good. And the way he

fucked me, seeking out all my pleasure spots like a missile, I clench a little between my legs as I drive home.

That night, even though I'm tender, I fuck myself with my dildo and attack my clit with my wand, trying to relive it. Damn. And this is just my first session with my first client. Maybe I'm not cut out for this after all, if I have to remain detached and professional in the face of... that.

Part of me hopes it didn't work this time. Our follow-up appointment is required, but after that, it's all dependent on the tests. Who knows how many more times I'll see him.

Will he eat me out like I'm a cake covered in icing again?

It's going to be a long month, I can already tell.

Luckily for me, I'm paid by DreamTogether for every moment after my first session. It felt absolutely fucking incredible to turn in my hat and uniforms to my creepy manager at McFlips, then say goodbye to the few coworkers I liked on the line.

I wonder how much of a bill the wolfman has rung up. Each breeding session costs him, and he's already paid the salary I'll make while I do nothing but sit around and incubate for however many months. It's not like I can ask him what he does for a living. The company was very straightforward in the handbook and paperwork about sharing any identifying details. We're under surveillance, too, for my safety—and surely they would hear it. Then I'd lose this job for good.

First thing the next morning, I make a list of everything I want to do now that I have the time. High up on the list is bingeing the next season of my favorite show, *The Golden*

Court. I haven't started it yet because I know it'll suck me in and I won't be able to stop until it's over.

Flipping on the TV, I look up some easy knitting patterns, then try my hand at it while the show plays. The sun rises higher in the sky, and I have some cereal, then remember the vitamin pills I'm supposed to be taking. The company was also pretty prescriptive about my diet, and I'm positive that having sugary cornmeal at II a.m. isn't what they had in mind.

I make a grocery list of healthy foods, using some recipes out of a cookbook that's collected a fine layer of dust, and head to the store. It's the middle of the day, so the aisles are clogged with old people and parents wrangling little kids while they try to shop.

Even though I'll be having a baby, that won't be my life. I'll go back to being single afterwards, which is kind of... freeing. Children are a lot of work, and I'm not sure I'm cut out for it.

But the wolfman sure thinks he's ready. And he must really, really want that for his life if he's going through this much effort to get it.

After shopping, I head home to make dinner, and pick something out of the recipe book. I don't cook a lot, usually easy stuff and microwave food, so this attempt at a healthy meal comes out... passable. That's being generous, actually, but I have confidence that I'll get better the more I do it.

I really want to have a glass of wine with my food, but that's literally and figuratively off the table now. I'll be allowed to imbibe during my three-month recovery period, but that's all.

Better find a new vice that isn't caffeine, either.

Late that night, I head back to the store again to pick up a box of Bubbles carbonated, flavored water, and wonder if I'm really doing the right thing.

Too late to back out now.

The following week, I go in for my first exam since the initial visit. I've managed to keep myself busy with knitting, watching television, going on long walks around my neighborhood and putting a tentative foot into gardening. I got a couple of planters for my balcony, and I'm giving it a try with some easy flowers and a basil plant. That's about as much responsibility as I can handle.

It's strange returning to the DreamTogether building, remembering what happened here last Thursday. I've been impossibly horny since then. Every night, sometimes multiple times during the day, too, I've laid down on my bed and played with my toys until I'm completely wrung out of orgasms.

I keep thinking about the wolfman's huge, furry hands, the claws in my flesh, the thick cock with that incredible knot at the base of it. I still don't know how he fit that thing in me, but damn, it was glorious. I don't think regular dick will be enough from now on.

I can have a personal life, of course. There's no prohibition against outside relationships or sex, but I have my doubts that too many people would be understanding about my chosen profession. Especially once I start to show, that option probably won't be on the table for me.

I think of the wolfman fucking me while I'm huge and pregnant, and I wish I didn't have to walk into a white, sterile doctor's office right now, probably so they can shove an ultrasound wand inside me.

Not hot.

We give perfunctory hellos, me and the middle-aged doctor with her hair up in a tight bun. She looks through my paperwork, then invites me to lie down and take off my clothes while she goes to get her supplies. I slide on the hospital gown, and wait until she comes back wearing a latex glove.

I hate this part. She looks around inside me with the wand, then makes some notes on a chart. Then she takes some blood to analyze and help me get better nutrition, and recommends some foods to me to get more potassium before sending me on my way.

It's too soon to know if it worked, but she reminds me to come in again next week for another check. I'll do it every week for the next who-knows-how-many months, until I'm finished and can go into recovery.

After my appointment, it's back to knitting, watching TV, walking, shopping, making meals... I manage to occupy quite a lot of my time, but there are still long periods where I don't quite know what to do with myself.

Maybe I should try to get out there and date before the whole pregnancy thing really sets in.

I call Liesel so we can catch up, and she meets me at a steakhouse. "I'm low on iron," I explain as we take a seat.

"Whatever. I know it's about the fried onion thing." She picks up her menu. "So, pregnant yet?"

She does love to get right to the point.

"I don't know," I say. "We still have one more appointment, and then they'll keep running tests until it comes up positive."

She nods as she browses the sides. "So what monster's baby are you going to carry around?"

I clear my throat. "A wolfman."

"Hmm." Liesel has one of those resting nothing-faces, where you can almost never figure out what she's thinking. I've learned her tells, though, over time, and I think she's a combination of curious and repulsed. "And you had sex with him?"

"Yeah, duh. That's the point."

She taps her cheek. "How was it?"

I don't have to think before I answer. "Really great," I say, trying not to sound *too* gushing, when actually it was mind-blowing.

Liesel quirks a brow. "I thought it was supposed to be a little more mechanical?"

"Not this guy," I say, tossing down my menu. "He was horny, and had amazing dirty talk. Except for the part where he gave me a fake name and it was Bill."

She makes a face, and I nod in agreement.

"Still, though, he knew just what to do," I add. "I came twice."

Liesel's watching me steadily. "Interesting. It's unusual for a man of any species to make a woman orgasm during their first time having intercourse."

"O-okay, Dr. Liesel," I say as the waiter approaches. "I guess he's just good at what he does." Though I do wonder just how he got so good at it. How many other women has he pleased that way? Were any of them human, too?

I'm surprised by a surge of jealousy.

I place an order for a rather large steak, and Liesel gets a salad. I don't know how she survives on just salads, but I decide to get one, too, and keep the healthy streak going.

"You know," Liesel says after the waiter leaves with our

order, "I've kept it to myself until now, but I wonder if this is the right move for you, Dee."

I frown at her. "Kinda late to say something." I could already be on my way to getting pregnant. I just imagine the wolfman's little army swarming up my fallopian tube toward the egg waiting for them there.

"I thought it would be all right," Liesel says cautiously, "but listening to you talk, I wonder if it's so healthy for you. You're emotional, and you love having connections with others."

That's odd, coming from her, because we have almost no friends in common. Liesel and I met at a music festival many years ago, and though other people in my life have cycled in and out, she's kept the same place, calling me every two weeks to get a drink. That's how I know she likes me, even if she never shows it. Over the years, I think we've built a strong bond, one where we understand each other and support each other.

"What, you think I'm going to get attached?" I ask, scoffing.

She just tilts her head. "Yes."

"You really have no faith in me." I guess I need to show her, then, that I can do this. Just because the wolfman took me for a ride, that doesn't mean I'm in it to win it. I'm only there to do a job.

If he wants to have fun doing it, that's fine by me.

Eventually the steak shows up, and I'm surprised by how hungry I am. I eat the entire thing, and wonder if soon I'll be eating for two.

Does that mean two steaks?

four

RUSS

FUCK.

This week is a drag. I've been working late shifts at the hospital, which doesn't put me in the best mood. And being away from my little human after such an intense moment of bonding is hitting me harder than I expected.

My kind are protective of their families, or so my dad was when I was little. But I knew that going into this. I simply thought I'd be better prepared to handle it.

I'm hard for her constantly. I manage to hide that fact under my loose scrubs, but my dick is there, lurking at half-mast while it ponders how it felt to be inside her.

I don't even know this woman and already I'm obsessed with her.

Still, I manage to focus on my work, because it's critically important that my patients have all of my attention. But each screaming infant I help bring into the world serves to remind me of what I'm after, what I want for myself.

It's hard to explain why I saved up the money to buy the full package at DreamTogether. There are probably plenty of other ways I could have gone about making a cub of my own. I've been married before, almost seven years ago now, but kids were the dealbreaker. Dating simply hasn't worked out since then. I'm thirty-six now, and I think it makes women suspicious that I've been single for so long.

They're right to be suspicious. I haven't felt a spark for anyone since Adelaine and I divorced. Hell, even before that. I knew she wasn't the one for me early on, but we'd already sealed the deal with rings and paper, so I stuck it out for as long as she would tolerate.

Eventually, though, she knew we wanted different things, so she took it upon herself to break it off.

I've realized since then that I don't need a partner. I'm content to do it by myself, and I've already worked out a deal with the hospital where I can work four days a week, regular shifts. We get discounted daycare, and then I'll have plenty of time to spend with the infant. I have a wet nurse already booked for the first two years of my new cub's life, to make sure they get everything they could possibly need.

It's the biggest expense I could have imagined, but I know what I want—and as soon as I heard of DreamTogether, I realized that's how I would get it.

But I didn't expect *her*. No, I didn't predict that the woman I would get would be designed for me, that she would call on my heart just like she did my cock. And I haven't even seen her face.

One week turns into two, and then two into three. I'm nearly vibrating with my need to have her again. I stand in the shower every morning and pump my cock hard, remembering how tight she was, how hard she squeezed me when she climaxed, and groan as thick spurts of white shoot out of me, painting the shower wall. Then I stand there, limp under the hot water, and pant until I can finish soaping off.

Can I really let her go after this is done?

I'm pleased when I get an automated call from DreamTogether telling me that my surrogate is ovulating again, and it's time for another visit.

I wake up much too early the next morning, my blood already pumping hard and fast. I'm more than eager to see her again, to slip my knot into her and fill her completely. I'm ready for her sweet moans, her unrestrained cries of pleasure, even her screams.

I did make her scream. I wonder if the other clients are able to do that.

This time, though, I have an ulterior motive. I'm going to try to gather what I can about her. Perhaps if I can get a hold of her phone number, or where she lives, or even just her real name, I'll be able to sniff her out.

I don't know if I can really let her go when this is all over.

By the time I reach the unmarked gray office building out on Cedar Road, my claws are gripping the steering wheel tightly. I manage to pull into a spot and climb out without scraping anything up, but I have to close my hands into fists when I head inside just to have somewhere to put the tension.

Fuck, my cock is hard as a rock already.

I talk to the receptionist through gritted teeth, and she gives me a funny look as she marks down that I've arrived. Then she heads off, popping my file into a holder on the wall.

There. That's where my female's information would be. I glance around the waiting room with its bright fluorescents and find two other monsters there—one big basilisk, his huge tail curled around two chairs. Then on the other end is a cyclops playing blocks with his toddler. I wonder if his child is from DreamTogether, too.

Great. Well, I can't peek at her file with others watching, but this won't be my last chance.

I sit back down and wait until the receptionist returns. She gestures first at the basilisk, then leads him away. I was late last time, so I made sure to come early this time. But I think I made it worse for myself because now I have to sit here and wait.

Finally, it's my turn, and I'm led to a different small, sterile room than the one where we met the first time. For a split second I panic, wondering if they're taking me to the wrong person, if there will be a different human woman waiting when I go in.

There's no way in hell I'm putting my cock in someone else.

I'm relieved when I walk in the door and find a familiar ass in front of me, raised up into the air by the bench. She's strapped down to it, which was a blessing last time when I absolutely ravaged her. I wonder if they had to throw all that rubber away because I destroyed it.

Instantly, the smell of her arousal hits me in the face, and the white tile walls vanish around us. If I wasn't hard before, I sure am now. All it takes is seeing her, breathing in a whiff of her, and I need nothing more than to fuck her again.

But I need to go slow. That's what a sensitive creature like her requires—lots of warming up, so she'll be soft enough to take my knot again. She's so small that I have to work up to it.

"Not nervous today, I see." I lick my chops, and her body twitches in response.

"Nope," she answers, keeping her eyes firmly ahead. I had rather hoped she'd try to look over her shoulder at me again, but it seems like she's trying to be more professional this time. "Welcome back, Bill."

That *name*. I'm such an idiot.

"What about you?" I ask as I approach her pert, round butt. It's nice and big, just like her wide hips, and great for groping. I run a finger over one soft cheek, and instantly her body twitches. "You call me Bill. What do I call you?"

Down below her little puckered ass, her pink slit is already opening and closing, pulsing with her need. So she remembers our last encounter as positively as I do. That's good.

"Me?" She sounds confused by the question. "What do you need it for?"

I lean down towards her, breathing against her exposed flesh. She trembles.

"So I can shout it while I'm fucking you," I say.

It's hard for me not to strip down right away and bury my dick in her again, but this time, I'm going to take my time, and see if I can weasel a detail out that might help me.

"O-oh," she says, clearly taken off-guard. "Well... you can call me Amanda."

I arch an eyebrow. Amanda. I don't think it fits her at all, but at least I know it's a fake name. She's wiser than to give out her real one under surveillance.

"Well, *Amanda*," I croon, extending my claws slightly to drag them down her ass. She gasps, and her pussy pulses again. The scent of her need is flooding my nose, filling up my snout and head. Damn, it's so good. "Are you ready for round two with the wolfman?"

She chuckles. "That's what you're paying me for, isn't it?"

I flinch at this. So she still sees it as just a gig. Didn't she like last time? She's giving me all the signals that she's excited for today.

"I suppose it is," I say carefully. "Do you like this job?"

"It's better than McFlips," she says, offhanded. But my heart leaps. There we go. A detail. I can use that.

"I see." I put my other hand on her, around her hip this time, and line myself up as if I'm about to drive myself into her sweet cunt. I'm still wearing my clothes, but the tent in my pants has grown significant, and increasingly difficult to ignore. "Still," I say, leaning forward to grind my clothed hips against her rear end, "that doesn't mean you can't like it."

She gasps, and manages to say, "That's t-true."

"And you did like it, didn't you?" I squeeze her bare flesh, and she wriggles. She's slick now, the lights reflecting off the shine on her swollen, pink cunt. I draw one knuckle down the cleft of her ass to her folds, and gently sweep through them. She bucks, pulling at her restraints, and I want nothing more than to fuck her so hard that she's screaming my name.

Well, Bill's name, anyway.

I drag her wetness down to her clit, circling it, not quite giving her what she's after. Amanda whimpers, pushing her hips against my hand, telling me to touch her.

"What do you want?" I ask her, gently teasing the tip of her nub, and then moving away from it so she squirms. "Do you want wolfman cock?"

"Yes!" She answers immediately.

"Too bad," I say, and crouch down to lick her.

Oh, she tastes so fucking good. She moans and lurches on the bench, moving away and toward me at the same time. She's already overstimulated, is she?

I press my tongue down on her clit, hard, and she cries out. Then I soothe it, lapping it slowly, before shoving it from side to side. Amanda whimpers, "Bill!" as she jerks her hips up. To reward her, I shove my tongue inside her.

It's easy to find that spot again, the one that made her gush last time. No human tongue could do this, but mine... I'll make sure she's never pleased by a human man again, not the way she is by me.

I stiffen my tongue and drag it across that spongy wall. She shudders instantly, her whole cunt fluttering. "Oh, Bill," she whines, rotating her hips to take even more of my tongue inside her. I scoop downward, bringing as much of her sweet fluid as I can into my mouth, and then I swallow it all. Once more I circle her clit, flicking over it and tormenting it until again...

She squirts right into my muzzle. I groan as she spills onto my tongue, and she lets out that worried gasp again. I soothe her with one palm on her ass.

"Thank you," I murmur, getting up to my feet. I sound collected and composed, but really, I can't take this anymore —I need to be inside her, or I might combust.

"You're thanking *me*?" Amanda asks, aghast. This time she does reflexively turn her head, and I catch sight of her pink cheek. "You just ate me out like a fucking professional."

I have to laugh, and I trail one claw down her back, from her shoulder blades over her shirt, to her bare hip. She shivers underneath me. With my other hand, I undo the buckle of my belt and unzip my pants, pulling them down to the ground.

I don't even bother with my shirt this time. I can't wait.

"Now that you've already taken me once," I say to her, palming my wet cock as it points directly toward her, "I won't be as gentle with you."

"Please." She wiggles her butt, and I drag my slick head through her spread pussy. "Don't be gentle, Bill."

Her unfiltered, carnal need is stoking a raging fire in me, one that demands I claim her. I'm still careful as I slide into her, but my way is much easier this time. Oh, her cunt remembers me, does it?

I will make sure she never forgets, too.

five

DEE

HOLY FUCK. I forgot exactly how good the wolfman felt. How his slippery cock, so unusually shaped, plies me open as it slides in. He reaches more than halfway on his first thrust, and he's so thick that I cry out. Groaning, he reels himself back, nearly leaving my body before he thrusts back in, deeper this time.

"Ohhh," I moan, falling forward on the bench. This is what I needed. This is what I've been practically bruising my clit trying to recapture. But nothing compares to this monstrous thing squeezing inside me, practically a physical impossibility, and yet...

"Ah, fuck, Amanda, you feel so good," my wolfman growls, reaching down to grip underneath the bench again. He's so much bigger than I am that his arms completely wrap around me. "Damn, your pussy is fucking amazing."

Wow. That's exactly the kind of thing a girl wants to hear. Each drive of his cock is pushing in deeper, and deeper, but never further than I can take it. He lowers his head to nuzzle underneath my braid.

"You like it, my dear?" he murmurs quietly, still moving with precise, slow strokes as he ventures farther into me with each pump of his hips. "You want all of my cock inside you?"

"Yes," I whimper, rather pathetically. "I want it. And your knot, too, Bill."

He groans on top of me, and his strokes speed up. He's gripping the bench even tighter now, so the whole thing rocks with each of his motions. Now he's truly deep, the thick lumps at the root of his cock making themselves known.

"Open up," he says, licking the bare skin at the nape of my neck. "Even your fucking sweat tastes great."

Why is that so erotic? I moan as his knot tries again to push through my wet pussy. Each stroke fires off another round of sparks, while the pointed head of his cock drags over something wonderful inside me. I'm so tight, so wound up, so swollen and yet those twin bulges are pushing their way in one thrust at a time. Soon it's most of the way inside me, and I'm no longer moaning, but screaming at how close my orgasm is. I'm sprinting towards the light, gripping my bench as tight as I can until I feel like I might simply burst open if I don't come.

"There we are," Bill murmurs in my ear as I shriek. "Give it to me, Amanda."

It's not my name, but I'm still fucking toast. My whole body climaxes, one immense shudder, and my voice completely stops in my throat. The wolfman growls something primal and deep, and shoves his huge knot through all my tightness, down deep where it belongs.

Where it *belongs*.

Then, just as my finish starts to wear off, he gets bigger.

That cock of his swells up even fatter, and my pussy riots. I come again, hard, harder than I ever have, and this time I scream. I clamp down tight around him, keeping that knot firmly wedged inside me.

We both pant, and droplets of his drool fall onto my back. He got so worked up for me that he can't control it. But my need has been growing for so long, so intensely, that my body wants even more.

As limp as I am, I manage to push my hips backwards, moving him inside me. The wolfman lets out a helpless moan, and actually drops some of his weight down onto my body.

"Wh-what are you—" he begins, and then I thrust my hips back again. He shatters. "Oh, Amanda."

"Do it again," I say harshly, because I'm desperate. I'm needy. And so what? I'll take what I can while I can, thank you.

Bill inhales sharply, and then slowly, raises himself back up. His huge hands find my ass, and he pushes even further inside me, letting out a tortured groan.

"I can't believe it," he mutters, more to himself than to me. "You're amazing, I... *fuck*." I'm so full of his come that it's making obscene, wet sounds as his knot starts to move back and forth inside of me, just a fraction of an inch at a time. But the sensation is so intense that I'm very quickly heading straight over the bridge again.

"So sensitive," Bill says as another tiny orgasm rocks my body. His knot has started to recede, so he gently withdraws it...

And then thrusts it right back in.

We go at it, my wolfman fucking me until I'm wailing, until my body is so overstimulated that all it takes is the rub of his knuckle on my clit to send me spiraling, again and again. Never did I expect this was possible, not on this planet, in this lifetime.

But when there comes a loud knock at the door, we both freeze.

"It's been more than an hour," an irritated voice calls. "Time to wrap it up."

Bill lets out a chuckle behind me. "I guess I had better come in you one more time," he says, trailing the tips of his claws down my spine. "And make sure it stays there."

I feel my mood dip at this thought. If we're successful today, which we surely will be, then we won't get to see each other again.

One last time, he unloads, and I'm so worn out I simply collapse against the bench. He drops down on top of me, knot secured, and rubs his face against the back of my head.

"I'm glad they chose you for me, Amanda," he says quietly. "You'll be such a good mother for my cub."

I know he means biological mother, not emotional one, but it still makes my heart lurch.

Maybe Liesel was right, and I made a huge mistake. But at least I'll get to keep part of him, for a while.

When his knot comes down, Bill gently pulls out, and covers my pussy with one hand. He leans forward, nuzzling his wet nose under my hair.

"*Amanda*," he whispers. I try to turn my head, because all I want is to tell him my real name, so this doesn't have to end. So he can come and find me out there. "What is—" he begins.

But then the door to the room flies open. "It's time," an angry voice says behind us. "Your session is over."

We went at it for so long that someone had to storm in and interrupt us just to make us stop. The attendant circles around to check on me in the restraints while the wolfman starts shuffling around like he's putting on his clothes.

He hisses a curse under his breath. With her here, there's no sharing details about our lives that might lead us back to each other again. Neither of us speaks as he's hurried out by the attendant, too aware of the cameras listening.

Eventually, the door opens again, and the wolfman departs. When he's gone, the attendant helps me down from the bench, and I'm red where I was pressed hard against the cushions, but I'm otherwise fine.

Though a lot of liquid does drizzle down my thigh when I get up.

I drive my car home in a kind of daze, a big, thick wall between me and my emotions. Something happened today, or maybe it was just part two of what started happening the first time we met in that sterile room.

There must be a way to contact him somewhere along the line. Maybe after the baby is born, I could have some kind of visitation, even if it's just to see Bill again.

But the moment I think it, I know there's no world in which that's allowed. It defeats the entire purpose, after all. He came to DreamTogether for a reason, for privacy, for no strings attached, and that's what he'll get with me if I want to keep this job. If I were to find out who he was, if I were to contact him outside the company, I would never get another chance at this. They would terminate me immediately upon the birth.

I park, then climb out and drift back to my dumpy apartment, to the planters where I've put my two flowers and my basil. They're already looking as wilted as I feel. Maybe I don't water them enough, or maybe I water them too much?

I head back inside and sit down on the couch, wondering what I do next while I wait. Signing up with DreamTogether had, well, looked like a dream come true for me. But now I'm here, simply hoping that I'll get to see Bill again.

I can't think like that. When this is over, we'll have nothing to do with each other.

Don't get attached.

RUSS

I don't hear anything after our second "session." One week passes, then two weeks. I hope that it didn't take. I know it's unlikely after how many times I pumped all my hot come into her, but I still hold out for the news that she's not pregnant yet, and I'll have to come back again.

Why did I leave without saying anything to her? Why did I let them hurry me out without at least getting her name?

Because I was drunk on her. Because there are eyes and ears everywhere inside DreamTogether, and I could have lost my chance completely at having a cub if I fucked it up.

I should have risked it anyway, for my woman. My *mate.*

After our experience together, I know it, in my bones and sinew. My blood pumps for her, my body craves her, my soul longs for her. But I don't know who she is, or where to find her.

Then I get the call. My heart plummets when I see the number on my screen.

"Yes?" I answer drearily.

"Mr. Cohen?"

"That's me."

"Congratulations!" I have to hold the phone away from

my ear. "We just received word that your surrogate is now pregnant. There will be no need for a third appointment."

For a brief moment I think that I won't have to shell out for an extra month on top of the whole package price I already paid. But what I wouldn't give right now to have that one extra visit.

At the mere idea that Amanda—or whoever she really is —my *mate*, is carrying my cub... all of my instincts come to life. I growl into the phone.

"I need her number," I say in a voice so low that even I don't recognize it.

"What?" The woman on the other end is silent for a moment. "Sir, you know we won't give that to you."

"*I need her number!*" I roar.

"And I need you to calm down," the woman says, now irritated. "You signed up for this. This is what you wanted. I promise, what you're feeling now will pass soon, and then all your dreams will come true."

That fucking tag line.

I smash the button to end the call and pace around my kitchen, then slam my fist into the stainless steel stovetop. The whole appliance shakes underneath me.

I must find her. I must protect her, and the new cub growing inside her. She's my everything, the pinnacle of my life. I was always meant to cross paths with her, to plant a cub in her, to make her mine.

Now I will keep them both safe from everything that might hurt them, if it's the last thing I do.

six

DEE

I STARE DOWN at the test like an idiot for far, far too long.

Two pink lines. A lot is going to change for me soon— but then, when it's all over, it will un-change, reverse, walk backwards until I'm back at the beginning again. Right in the same place, with some other monster's baby.

A shudder rolls down my spine at the idea of doing what we did with anyone else. No, that's reserved. It would never be like that, it *couldn't* be like that.

At the same time, knowing that I'm carrying the wolf-man's kid? I feel almost... warm inside. I'm already imagining the two of us, combined into a single embryo, the new life we created steadily growing inside me.

I drop the test into a plastic baggie, and stare at it a while longer. That stranger is now in my body, a permanent testament to the wonderful, wild encounter we had in that sterile room.

I wish it could have been somewhere else, somewhere we

could have taken our time, maybe even looked at one another. What would it be like to have Bill in a bed, surrounded by his arms?

I'll never know. And that's probably for the best.

When I make the call to DreamTogether about the positive test, I'm brought in right away for a medical exam. After confirming with blood samples and ultrasound that I am, in fact, pregnant, the doctor walks me through the steps.

I'll gestate for approximately ten months, somewhere between the human nine and the wolf-people's eleven. The baby might be a little bigger than the average human baby, but in the data the doctor found, not by much. It shouldn't be a difficult pregnancy or labor—not more than usual, anyway.

Fuck. *Labor.* I don't know why that had seemed so far off when I signed my name on the dotted line, but now it's looming in front of me like a towering tidal wave, ready to smash down in ten months' time.

On that bench, in that white room with Bill, was the moment my life veered to one side. Whatever flame had sprouted between us when we met, it's become a bonfire. Now Bill the wolfman is the only thing on my mind. A complete stranger to me, whose face I've never even seen, is now the person who occupies most of my waking hours. It's stupid, really, to fantasize and obsess over someone I'll never see again, someone who I really only know because we fucked a couple times.

I would be lying to myself, though, if I said that's all it was. But it can never be anything else, anything more than our two momentary collisions at DreamTogether. The company made sure of that. I don't know who he is, and he'll never know who I am.

Those are the rules. And I can't even drink to wash it away.

After the doctor's appointment, when all my results have been confirmed, I slog back to my apartment feeling heavy. I knew I'd be doing this completely on my own, but facing it is different. At least I have Liesel. Maybe she'll come over and watch a movie.

When I walk in the door, I find the state of my home even more depressing. What an ugly place. Sitting on that couch in the dark corner, pregnant and watching television, sounds like someone should be calling CPS on me.

So the first thing I do is stalk back out into the hall, knock on my super's door, and give him my notice. I have the money to do it now, so I'm getting the fuck out of here.

Even if it's not born yet, my kid deserves a good life, and so do I.

RUSS

McFlips. That's where Amanda used to work, I'm sure of it. And she quit recently, too, which will help.

But there are a lot of McFlips in the human city of Aston, and it'll take me a while to inquire personally at each of them.

I have nine, maybe ten months to figure it out. That's plenty of time. Whether I can hold my shit together that long and not bulldoze DreamTogether just so I can contact her... that's the question.

When my shift at the hospital is over for the night, I start at the first McFlips on the edge of town. It's the seediest one, and I hope that this isn't the place she worked.

It's late, almost 1 a.m., but that could be a good thing. Perhaps she was on the night shift.

I have to endeavor not to slam the glass door of the fast food restaurant when I storm in. I'm dying to see her already, even though I only got the news about our cub last night. The human clerk at the counter glances up with wide eyes when I come in, as if he was just asleep, and he was certainly not expecting to see a wolfman when he woke up.

"Oh, good evening, and—" He yawns. "—welcome to McFlips. What can I do for you?"

I lean forward across the counter, very close to him, so close he has to tilt back. The guy's mouth falls open.

"A girl," I say, a growl to my voice. "A girl worked here. Black hair in a braid. Quit two months ago or so."

He blinks. "N-no girl has quit recently," he says, clearly shaken. I wonder how many monsters he sees out here. "Not since I've been here. Though turnover is high in the service—"

I cut him off. "Are you sure? Not even on the day shift?"

He rapidly shakes his head. "Not that I know of."

I reel back from the counter and turn around, striding out of the building as quickly as I entered it. Maybe I understand better now why Amanda took the job at DreamTogether, if this was the kind of place where she spent all of her days.

At least that was quick, so I can get to the next one.

43

Unfortunately, the following stop proves to be just as fruitless. There are about 250,000 people in Aston, and four different McFlips just within city limits. She might not even live in Aston, I realize as I drive towards the next one in the dark. She might live in one of the smaller towns outside of it, farther from DreamTogether.

Fuck. I didn't think of that. That adds at least another three or four locations to my list.

The second stop is even less useful to me, because the two employees behind the counter aren't sure who works the day shift. It looks like I'll have to come back again in the morning, so I buy a burger and leave.

I decide to go home and get some shut-eye before I have to be back at the hospital tomorrow. There are a couple of planned C-sections, and who knows what else might come up.

I fall asleep hearing Amanda's cries as I plunge into her, and hoping I'll pick up her scent again soon.

I'm exhausted by the end of my shift at the hospital the next day, but I'm still intent on carrying out my search. There are three more McFlips to hit in the city and find out what I can about Amanda. Part of me hopes that if I can even pick up just a hint of her smell, I might be able to track her down. It's a long shot after so much time has passed since she quit, but you never know.

The first place I stop, the swing shift manager is working the counter. He cheerily asks what I'd like to have.

"A friend of mine quit a McFlips a couple months ago," I

begin. "She said she left a pin in one of her uniforms. She really loved that pin but has given up on it."

The manager thinks. "Hmm, there was someone who quit just a couple weeks back, but she was like, forty. How old is your friend?"

I have to think about this, and the manager starts to look suspicious. "It was her birthday last week," I explain. "I'm trying to remember if she's twenty-eight or twenty-nine."

"Definitely not the woman who quit, then," he says, and I want to flip over the whole counter. "Sorry."

I clench my hands into fists and manage to keep from letting out a roar of frustration. I give him a quick nod and stride out, then once I'm in the parking lot, I howl a long, mournful howl. A couple in the parking lot quickly dart away and head for the door.

I try the same gag at the next McFlips, but they haven't lost any employees recently. I'll have to come check these places again during the day, I decide, because I didn't trust the young girl behind the counter to have even been around long enough to know if Amanda worked there or not.

When I get back to my house, I feel like I could pass out at the wheel. I stop in front of my gate and lean out the window of my car, then push the code. The gate groans as it opens, and I think that I should probably come out here with some WD-40 and take care of that.

I haven't been able to hire anyone for anything around the house since I started saving up for DreamTogether, and it shows. The lawn has grown wild, but I manage to avoid HOA penalties because of my gate and the hedges. None of the flowers came up this year, and the yard is simultaneously withering and out of control.

The inside isn't much better. I've been working so many hours that all self-care has gone out the window, from

cleaning up my dishes to sleeping enough to getting exercise. I have a treadmill in my big bedroom, right in front of
the second-story windows, but it's covered in dirty laundry
and stretching bands I don't use.

If I had someone like Amanda around, I would never
have let it become like this. I just have no reason to do better
when I'm the only one living here, not even a cat or a pet
hamster in sight.

I sigh and flop down in one of the living room chairs.
This is one of the only clean rooms, simply because I never
use it.

I suppose for the sake of the cub, I should get my act
together. I'll have to do a lot better than this if I'm going to
become a full-time father in a matter of months.

But for now, I need some fucking sleep.

seven

RUSS

I HAVE an entire twenty-four hours off today, and I'm going to use every last bit of it.

I return to each of the McFlips locations I've already visited and ask their daytime staff the same question, spinning the same lie. Still, no sign of her.

On to the next one. Even worse than a positive "no" is the two kids behind the counter shrugging, saying they're college students who just started a week ago. The manager isn't interested in answering my questions, either, as he's much too busy wrangling his underage staff.

Great.

Up until the fourth stop, I'm driven fully by my need to find Amanda, to make sure she and my cub are all right. It sprouted as a primal urge, but when I pull into the parking lot, it's morphed into a resigned frustration.

What if I can't turn up any leads at all? The weight of the time ahead, wondering and waiting while my mate grows my cub, sinks down on my shoulders like a stone.

Fuck. I can't give up already.

I get out of the car, slam the door, and walk into the McFlips. It's on the nicer end of town, with cleaner tile floors. Aston is a predominantly human city, but most of the diners politely try not to stare as I walk in.

I take a deep breath, searching for a whiff of her. For a moment, I almost think I can pick it out, but then it vanishes just as quickly.

"Can I help you, sir?" asks an older woman behind the counter. Her tag says MARIAN.

"Sure, please." I study the menu for a moment. "I'll have a double bacon cheeseburger. But I'd also like to ask you something? Um, Marian?"

She tugs up her visor and peers at me from under graying curls. "What's that, sir?"

I smooth back the wild fur around my cheeks. "Look," I say, tired of all the pretenses. "I'm searching for someone. A woman I... a woman I slept with. A couple of weeks ago."

Marian's eyes go wide. Then, a slight smile tugs at the corner of her lip. "Go on."

I lean forward so I don't have to speak as loudly. "It was really amazing. But we didn't exchange information." It's about as close to the truth as I can get without spilling the sordid details of the strangers-fucking-in-a-white-room situation. "She said she worked here a few months back, and I just..." I trail off, hoping I'm not about to wreck my chance of getting an answer. "I want to see her again. More than anything."

That smile spreads, and Marian's eyes crinkle. "I see." She calls back over her shoulder. "Jason, I'm taking my break."

"It's not time for your break!" A scrawny man leans

around the corner, face pink with pimples. He has a tag that says MANAGER.

"My feet hurt," Marian answers as she heads away from the counter. She waves at me, urging me toward the door that leads behind it.

The manager sighs and vanishes.

When I reach the side door, she opens it for me and ushers me in.

"Don't let anyone see you," she says, which is a rather big ask of a giant wolfman inside a fast food restaurant.

She leads me down a hallway to another small room, and I have to hunch down to fit through the door. There, she goes to a cabinet and opens it.

"You want her number, right?" Marian asks.

"Or her address," I say. "I just want to leave her flowers or something. I feel like that's less intrusive than calling out of the blue."

She rubs her chin. "True." She leafs through the files. "Here we go. Deanna Jackson."

Deanna. That's her name. That's Amanda's *real* name. It sounds much more... right for her.

And it feels like I'm finally a step closer.

"She went by Dee, by the way," the woman says with a knowing arch of her brow. "Since I assume you didn't get her name, either."

I sheepishly shrug. "Thank you," I say, fully sincere. "This means a lot to me."

She pulls out the file and grabs a notepad, quickly copying down the address. "You'd better not be some creep ex-boyfriend, though," she says in a warning tone.

I raise my hands in the air. "No, I'm not, I promise." I swallow, not sure if I should say what I'm really thinking.

Marian tears off the paper with the address but doesn't hand it to me.

"Would you give me the number, too?" I ask, knowing that I'm pushing my luck. I just want a back-up, just in case.

Marian frowns. "I don't think I should," she says, now uncertain. "I probably shouldn't even be giving you this—"

Before she can finish her sentence, I snatch the piece of paper with Dee's address right out of her hand.

She huffs with indignation. "Sir!"

"Sorry," I tell her, heading for the door. At least I was able to get this much. It should be enough to locate Dee. "You don't understand, but I have to find her."

Then I rush back out the way I came in.

My heels are practically on fire as I hop into my car and turn on the navigation. I type in the address and then hit GO.

My GPS leads me deeper into Aston, back toward the seedy end of town. It's only a few minutes to the apartment complex, which is rundown and falling apart on the outside. The stairs are rickety, and she's up on the second floor.

I don't like that hazard. She could lean too hard on the railing and tip right off the side if I'm not there to watch out for her.

Fuck. Danger is everywhere in the world. I don't know why I thought I could handle this.

I park in the lot, which is on an unsettling slope, and step out. That one should be hers—number four. Navigating my way up the slope to the old, haphazard stairs, I find they're just cement blocks laid down with big gaps between them.

Not safe at all.

I reach the top floor and walk across the landing to the apartment marked with a "4." Then I slowly raise one knuckle and knock.

I might be doing something really, really stupid right now. Maybe Amanda—no, *Dee*—was silent after our second session because she really didn't want me to know who she was.

That was what we signed up for, isn't it?

But it's too late. I've knocked, and I hear footsteps on the other side of the door headed towards me.

The knob turns, and the door opens.

The man who answers it is wearing an apron and carrying a bucket of water. He scowls at me.

"What?" he demands. The apartment behind him is...

Completely empty.

"Deanna?" I ask. "Deanna, uh, Jackson?"

The man squints at me. "Do I look like a Deanna?" he snaps.

"No, no." I wave my hands. "I'm trying to find her."

The man looks me up and down, from my bare, clawed feet to my pointed ears.

"No girl named that here," he says pointedly, gesturing at himself. "Maybe she's the one who moved out. I don't know, and I don't care." He shoos me, and promptly slams the door closed.

I stand on the landing, staring at the "4" that hangs slightly off to one side. I right it, and realize that my hand is trembling.

I expected her to be here. I expected to see her again.

Immediately I pull out my phone and start looking up the property. It's managed by a rental company, as I expected, so I call them as I head back down the stairs to my car.

At least she isn't living *here* anymore.

"Hello, Muer Real Estate Management."

"Hello, hi," I say, tapping the handle of my car door to unlock it. "I'm looking for an address. My friend just moved, and I'm..." What, I'm trying to find her? That doesn't sound suspicious at all. "I'm trying to forward her mail, but I don't know her new address. I know how to find the damn place, but that's it."

"Right," says the woman on the other end. "Sorry. I don't have that. Once our business is concluded with a renter, it's up to them to have their mail forwarded."

I gawp at the phone. "Really? You don't ask them for a future address?"

"No. Is that all?"

I can't fucking believe it. I end the call and shove the phone into my pocket as I slide back into my car.

A hard, abrupt dead end.

DEE

Finding a new apartment is more difficult than it sounds. Eventually I do locate a nice place, right at the top of my price range, that's a little farther outside of Aston than my old spot. It's not like I have to commute anywhere, so a bright, high-ceilinged loft in a bedroom community sounds perfect for me. Once I've packed up everything I own, I call as many friends as I can to help move it all, and buy them pizza at the end of the day. It's when I do one last check of the empty apartment, vacuuming in some of the corners, that I realize that I'm not just saying goodbye to this dump of a place.

I'm saying goodbye to my old life, too. I don't know if that's a good thing or a bad thing, but it's now happening at full speed.

At the last minute, I remember my planters on the balcony, and take them with me.

I spend a lot of time that first week in my new place getting everything unpacked and arranging it just-so. I've never had the time or energy for decorating, and I don't have much to decorate *with*, but I do make a run to the secondhand store that results in some tacky sculptures, weird paintings and extra furniture. Then I find new homes for my plants on the back porch, and even pick up a shiny new silver watering can.

But once everything is all hung and placed... I realize just how fucking lonely my life is without a job.

I don't mind the *not having a job* part. It's nice not to force myself to go to sleep, or wake up at an ungodly hour in the morning when my alarm goes off. It's wonderful not to stare longingly up at the clock for my shift to be over. In fact, after a few days, I'm setting an alarm voluntarily so I don't over-sleep and feel groggy all day.

Still, I wish I could teleport my good coworkers right to my house and just... do things together. It's boring being by myself at my house all the time, even if the new apartment has far better mojo than my last one did. I can't see Liesel every single day, and my other friends either have kids or work long hours. They make time for me when they can, but it's not much compared to the hours alone.

It's not that I'm bored. It's that everything feels too quiet. As the days go on, the quiet grows deeper and deeper, and I wonder if I might get sucked into it.

I seriously need to get out more. I don't care if I have to go to a bar and sip virgin cocktails to have a conversation with someone. Hell, even if all I do is watch the game while surrounded by strangers, that's good enough for me.

Maybe Liesel was right, and I do crave connections. Maybe all of this was a really dumb idea.

It's a little harder to find a good lounge spot outside of the city, but I do manage to locate a bar and grill nearby that seems more focused on the "bar" part. Perfect. I could use some deep fried food since I've been eating healthy *salads* all the time.

The bar is dim inside, with a few chunky pendant lights hanging above the bartop and tables. It has a homey feel to it, different than the trendy bars in the city where a cocktail costs fifteen bucks. This reminds me more of my hometown, where every bar looks and smells just like this one, and you can order a side of mozzarella sticks to go with your cold beer.

Almost everyone in the bar is human, save for a pair of fish-men over by the jukebox arguing over what to play next.

"What would you like?" the bartender asks the moment I sit, while she's filling a beer glass.

"A virgin cocktail," I say. "Any kind."

She arches her eyebrow, opens her mouth to say something, then closes it and nods. "I can respect that," she says. "Preferences?"

"None." She departs to drop off the full beer, then grabs some jars and a pitcher of orange juice out of the fridge. She mixes things together like a mad scientist, then slides an orange and pink drink in front of me.

"Not sure what to call it, but I think it'll be good." Then she's gone to help another customer.

There's no one sitting next to me, but two seats down on

my left is a man in my age range, swishing his beer while he watches the game. I study him, trying to decide if I find him attractive or not. He has an okay face, but nothing to write home about. He's probably about the same amount of attractive I am. That's a positive sign.

The cure to loneliness is to hook up, I'm pretty sure of it. Maybe if I can just get some tonight, I'll stop longing for wolfman cock to such an embarrassing degree.

I lean over to get a better look at the TV. It's a Broncos game, and the man doesn't look particularly interested. Good. Just like me.

Eventually he spots me looking at him, and turns his head to make full eye contact. I don't waver, but I do offer a smile.

"Not that exciting of a game?" I ask, glancing at the television and back.

He shrugs. "I'm just not invested." He has greenish-brown eyes and short, brown upswept hair. He's dressed like he came here after work, with a collared shirt and slacks. "Which team are you here for?"

I shake my head. "Neither. Rarely watch football, actually. I'm not even sure what the rules are."

He laughs, which is a good start. "So why are you here by yourself?" He glances down at my drink. "Screwdriver?"

"I don't know. Something the bartender made up." I take a sip, trying to decide how much to say. "I just needed to... be around people for a while."

The stranger cocks his head. "Are you alone a lot?"

"All the time." I swish my drink and sip it again because I'm starting to sweat. It's been a minute since I tried to hit on someone, and I'm rusty. "It gets old after a while."

But it's not just the need to have company. It's the hunger

for *Bill's* company, specifically, and the odd void it's left behind in me.

"And a seedy bar is what does it for you?" the man asks, skeptical.

I hold up my drink. "And virgin cocktails, too."

Another laugh, and I think perhaps my charms are working. "I won't ask why," he says. "None of my business. But I guess a bar is a good place to be if you don't want to be... alone."

He smiles as he says this, and I know I've caught him.

eight

DEE

"OH, FUCK," I moan, trying to make it seem like I'm really enjoying myself. Robbie, the guy I've brought home with me from the bar, is naked and sweating underneath me, propped up against my headboard. He plays with my tits while I rise up again on his cock, then slide back down.

It's just not the same. Not at all.

And that isn't only because of the condom. He doesn't fill me up the way Bill did, with that strangely-shaped dick of his. Unfortunately, that was perfect.

Robbie is fine, for a human guy. He's moderately attentive to my pleasure, and when he gets close to coming, he reaches down between my legs to play with my clit.

It's still incredible that Bill could make me come with just his cock.

I rock back and forth in Robbie's lap, but my legs are starting to get tired. This isn't doing it for me.

"Hey, hey," I say, falling all the way down on his cock so he groans. "Doggy style me?"

Robbie blinks a few times, then nods. "Okay, sure." I awkwardly climb off him and get on my hands and knees. I imagine I'm strapped down to the bench again, my legs spread, my feet in the stirrups. I can almost hear a growl behind me as Bill walks up to position himself.

Robbie slides in, and I hate the feel of the condom between us. Here, at least, I can touch my own clit, and I do so as he fucks me faster and harder.

"Oh, damn," he moans. I want him to say something else, to say something dirty like Bill did, but he just grunts as I get closer and closer to my very distant climax.

Finally, I'm there, and Robbie lets go. At least he waited for me. That's somewhat impressive.

Maybe, if I can just open my mind to it, this dating thing could work out. It's a matter of when I tell him the truth.

Robbie stays the night, but we don't really cuddle. It didn't feel intimate, what we did—it was more like a necessary bodily function. I don't sleep that well, either, with someone else in my bed.

The next morning, though, the stranger I picked up at the bar is affectionate, even as he puts on his clothes quickly to get to work on time. He comes up to me as he buttons his jeans and kisses me on the lips.

"Do I get your number?" he asks in a purr. "That sex last night was incredible."

At least it was incredible for one of us. But maybe dating this guy could be fun, and get my mind off of Bill.

"Sure. Only if you actually call, though." I pull out my phone, and he pulls out his.

"Of course I'll call." He squeezes my ass. "Not every day some hot woman in a bar takes you home with her."

I can't tell if I like him, or if I like that he likes me. We exchange numbers anyway, and then with another kiss, he's gone.

But I still feel empty inside, like I found a band-aid to cover a wound that will never heal.

RUSS

I sit on my couch, my head in my hands, listening to the television blare.

I lost the trail.

The scent of her arousal still hangs in my nose, but it's fading slowly. I hope I don't forget it.

No. I'll never forget it. Not as long as I live.

I haven't even caught a whiff of Dee since I went to that empty apartment. Maybe she moved away. What if she left the state completely? How would I find her then?

Damn. I need a drink.

All it takes is a text message to my friend Caleb to get me out of the house. He's barbecuing, he says. He has some cold ones and hot dogs if I come over now.

A few of our friends have gathered in Caleb's backyard, and they all raise their beers when I arrive. I wonder if any of them had planned to invite me.

Marlene trots over with her drink clasped in her claws. She extends her huge, feathery wings, then parks them again against her back.

"Good to see you up and about," she says, welcoming me into the grassy backyard.

"Up and about?" I ask. "I'm always up and about. I work in a hospital."

"Yeah," chimes in Caleb, "but besides that, you just mope around."

Is that why they're all meeting up without me? Because I'm a bummer?

"Wow, guys," I say, tossing back some beer. "Good to know I have my friends' support."

Caleb blinks his huge, single eye at me. "Of course you have our support. But you didn't really want it, friend. Every time we asked you to come out with us, you said no."

I guess that's true. I just didn't... feel like it.

Maybe it was better to sit around and mope, wondering what Dee was doing out in the world. How is our cub growing? Early pregnancy can be unpleasant and uncomfortable —as can the rest of the process of creating another person— and I want more than anything to be there with her.

"Just hand me a beer," I say instead, holding out one paw. Caleb rolls his eye and heads for the cooler, grabbing a bottle and tossing it to me. I snap the lid off with my claw, then throw it back.

Ah, that's good. Just what I needed: a beer and some sunshine. Now, if only it were a raw deer instead of a hot dog...

I haven't gone hunting in a long time. Maybe I should rectify that. Some blood on my face and a still-beating heart in my mouth might just be exactly what the doctor ordered.

A different doctor. I just do babies.

"I guess you didn't have any luck tracking her down?" asks Marlene, pushing back some of the feathers on her head.

"Dead end," I say. "Now I have no idea where to look."

"Well, you know her name. Just scope her out on social media."

"I did that." She didn't have much of a presence, all be told. Some old photos from college, and a professional profile that was wildly out of date. I get the sense she tried to find a good job after graduating, but didn't have any luck and ended up at McFlips. "Not enough to go on. No friends in common."

Marlene *hmms*. "You could do it the old-fashioned way and hire a PI."

I stare at her. "A private investigator? Really?"

She shrugs. "Why not? That's why they exist."

I'd be expressly going against DreamTogether's policies if I hired someone to help me find her. But I'm not above it at this point, either.

"What could a PI do that I can't?" I ask.

"Maybe get her forwarding address? They're the professionals, not me."

I spend the rest of the barbecue chewing over her suggestion. It might be exactly the thing I need. Because the instinct to find Dee, to watch over her, is all-consuming.

The first chance I get, I start searching for private investigators. Though most look like spam sites, a few locals pop up. I call each one, but two of the three say they aren't taking new work.

The third one, a young-sounding woman, hums on the other end of the line when I ask her rates.

"Tell me what you're after, and then I tell you how much

it costs," she says, and I can hear her tapping a pen on a desk.

"I'm trying to find a woman," I say.

"I knew that already."

I huff. "A woman who's carrying my child. A human woman."

There's a momentary silence, and then: "And you don't know her?"

"I do know her. I just... don't know where she lives, or how to get in touch with her."

The PI hums thoughtfully on the other end of the line. "Interesting conundrum. Okay. I don't ask details because I don't care. I generally try to keep out the axe murderers, but I think you're just after your kid. That will cost you four grand."

I pull the phone away from my ear and stare down at it.

"Four *grand*?"

"What did you expect to pay? This is my living. Now cough it up, or this call can be done."

She's a real ball-buster, and it reminds me of Dee.

"Fine."

"Fax over the information," she says, "and I'll see if I can help you."

A fax machine? I must be living in the wrong decade.

She rattles off the number and promptly hangs up. I write down what I can about Deanna, including her old address and place of work. Then I trudge down to the local print shop to see if they can get me to a fax machine.

A few minutes later I get another call.

"Cash only," the PI says without introduction. "And I'll find your baby momma."

"Done."

I hope I'm not throwing my money away, but it's worth it if it gets me even a little closer to finding Dee.

DEE

The morning after picking up Robbie at the bar, I go after my knitting more vigorously. I thought he would be the perfect distraction, but now I have a gnawing feeling in the pit of my stomach. Whatever hunger was sated by last night, it was surface level, and now the need is back even worse than before.

To distract myself, I put on nature documentaries that might be somewhat educational, and that way I don't feel like I'm simply wasting my day away watching soaps.

Though I do love soaps.

I work my way up some complicated patterns, but then my eyes and my hands get tired, so I go on a long walk around the neighborhood to fill the time. I'm even more restless now, like something is missing.

Maybe I should get a dog. Then at least I'd look like I have a reason to be out walking all the time.

Then the dog makes me think of Bill, and I just want to kick a trash can. Why didn't I offer him my number at the end of our second session? I could have whispered it in his ear, so no one could overhear.

Okay. The dog. The dog is a good idea.

I immediately pull up the shelter on my phone, and look through the pictures of available dogs. One face stands out at me, a hound-like animal with floppy ears and big jowls. His bio says that he's an older dog, but still needs plenty of walks.

He sounds perfect for me.

I call on my way home and make an appointment to go and meet "Boomer." I'll need to get my landlord's permission, but it shouldn't be too hard.

Yeah. Maybe that's exactly what I need. A dog and a fuck buddy to keep me company until this baby comes out, and I can try to pretend like Bill never happened.

That's a lot easier said than done when the morning sickness sets in.

I thought it would come on sooner, and then I could get it over with, but nope. And it's not just in the morning, either. I'll suddenly feel nauseated while I'm eating cereal—yes, still eating cereal—and sprint to the bathroom, puking up all my guts. Or it'll happen at night when I'm getting ready for bed.

I have issues with whoever called it *morning* sickness. It's just *sickness sickness*, and it fucking sucks. Even worse is knowing this is just the beginning.

I have all the books. I've already bought special inserts for my shoes for later, when I'm too big and my feet start to hurt. I have the heating pads for my back, and the creams for my stretch marks. I know I won't escape without a few of those, but I don't mind. I'll wear them like a tattoo.

Robbie does call me, like he promised, and I tell him I'm going to meet a dog.

"You really are lonely," he says. "Want some company? I have the day off."

I guess I wouldn't mind bringing someone with me who maybe knows more about dogs than I do, so I agree.

We meet at the shelter, and to my surprise, Robbie kisses me there in the parking lot. I already have a feeling he's more into this than I am, but that could be a good thing. When I tell him the news, maybe he won't go running for the hills.

Inside, the shelter is overrun with loose cats. Good thing I'm not allergic. I check in at the front desk, and the young man behind the counter leads me to a meeting room. "I'll bring Boomer here," he says, and leaves us alone.

"Do you have a yard?" Robbie asks as we sit on the couch, a polite distance between us.

"No, just a balcony. But there's a greenway right outside the building, and it's not like I have anything else to do all day."

I probably shouldn't have said that, but eventually he'll find out I don't have a regular job. If we keep doing this.

He squints at me. "Are you independently wealthy or something?"

I laugh and shake my head. "That would be great, but no. I just have a weird job."

He's about to ask me more when the door opens, and a big, lumbering giant comes in. The dog is brown all over, with a kind, gentle face. He trots over to greet me right away, and his huge tongue swipes down the side of my face.

He'll be perfect for me.

nine

RUSS

FOR THE TWO weeks I don't hear from the PI, I could tear holes right in the wall. I don't, of course. I don't have the time, energy, or money to have that fixed after digging through my meager savings for four grand.

The wait is agonizing. Instead of avoiding my friends, I deluge them with invitations to get out of the house so I can think about something else for a few minutes. I wonder if the PI is taking so long because she hasn't had any luck yet, and Dee will be even harder to track down than I thought.

Then, one night, a familiar number calls me. I hurriedly pick up the phone.

"Did you find her?" I say, without even a greeting.

"Why, hello to you, too," the PI says, with what is most definitely a smirk in her voice. "The answer is a little more complicated than that."

Uh oh. I don't like the sound of this.

"Well, do you know where she is, or not? I feel like it's pretty simple."

She sighs through the phone. "Your girl, whether accidentally or not, is pretty hard to find. I have her car model, make, and license plate number, but she hasn't updated her address on her driver's license yet."

"So you have nothing for me?" My paw curls into a fist, and I clench my teeth together. "After four grand and two weeks?"

The PI huffs. "Cool down. I'm calling to let you know I'm still on the trail. Now that I've found the car, I can keep my eyes peeled for it. And I got some other clues about her. She has a friend who has a much bigger presence online, and I think I can use her to find Deanna."

So that's why it's taking so long. She's waiting for someone else to lead her to Dee.

"So how much more time, do you think?" I try to sound calm as I ask it, but I feel anything but calm. The fur on my mane is standing on end, and my tail is thrashing back and forth behind me.

"Working as hard and fast as I can," she says, though her tone is bored. "I'll get back to you as soon as I have something. Keep your britches on, wolfman."

With that, she hangs up, and I shove my phone back into my pocket. Humans.

I wonder who this friend is, and if she'll be able to get me to Dee.

Dee, with her long black braid hanging over her shoulder. I remember her soft, broad hips, and perfect round ass. I can almost feel it under my claws again.

Which leads me, inevitably, to her squeezing pussy, and then fuck, I'm hard as a rock.

Right there in my kitchen, in front of my big glass windows, I unzip my pants and pull out my cock. It's leaking for her, just thinking about being inside her again, imagining her cries. With an agonized groan, I jerk one out, and after I've splattered all over the floor I do it again, just remembering how she wanted me to fuck her over, and over, and over.

I know I will never find anyone else like her, like my *mate*, ever again.

I have to find her. I can't wait any longer to learn where she is, how she's doing, whether the cub inside her belly is well and safe.

Fuck. I have to know. I will destroy the world just to get to her.

Miraculously, though, I gain some post-nut clarity. This friend of hers... if I could just smell her, I would know if she'd been with Dee recently. Then I could track the scent back to Dee's home.

Yes. That's the answer. Maybe I don't need this human PI after all when I have my nose at my disposal. I just need someone to get me closer, to dangle a scrap of clothing in front of my face and I can do the rest myself.

I pull out my phone and quickly call the PI back.

"I need whatever information you've found already," I tell her. "Right now."

After trucking down to the prickly young woman's office to get a copy of her documentation, I sit outside the office building of one Liesel Monahan, waiting for her to emerge for the day. My shift starts later tonight, and I should probably be sleeping—but finding my cub and its mother is my top priority right now.

Once I know they're safe, I can relax.

I almost nod off while waiting, but then I catch a head of white-blonde hair leaving the office building. There. She looks just like the driver's license photo the PI gave me.

I hop out of my car and, without any fear at all in me, I stalk towards her. I have a plan, even if it's a half-assed one.

Her face gives nothing away as I approach, even though monsters aren't common in this part of town.

"Can I help you?" she asks, slinging her briefcase over her shoulder.

"I'm... trying to find someone in this building," I say. "Mister, um, McJenkins. Do you know which floor I could find him on?"

While she surveys me, still silent, I breathe in a big whiff of her. *There.* I have it. It's Dee's smell, still faint and twisted up with many other smells, but there. My heart leaps. It fucking *soars*, and greedily I inhale again to savor that familiar musk.

"There's no Mr. McJenkins here," Liesel says coolly, looking me up and down. "I think you're at the wrong place."

I hum thoughtfully, but inside, I'm turning over how best to accomplish what I need to accomplish. How to get to my woman.

"Maybe not. I thought this was the right address." I pull out my phone and pull up the map.

"I'm sure you did," she says, tilting her head curiously at me. "What's your name?"

Great. I'm not so good at acting, I guess.

"Oops," I say instead, pretending that I've just found the right location on my phone. "I guess he's in the next building over. My apologies."

"Hm," is all Liesel says, before she walks away, and I suck in another blissful, tormenting whiff of Dee before she's gone.

Once Liesel has returned to her car, I go back to mine. I wait until she pulls out of the lot, and then I do the same, making sure to keep another car between us. Her little sedan is easy to follow, mostly because she drives like an old lady. I almost want to honk at her to get her out of my way.

As she reaches her house, I take a right turn and park on an adjoining street. I get out and watch as she pulls into her garage and then closes the door behind her.

With the way now clear, I jog across the road. A woman walking her dog on the neighboring block stops to stare at me, and I give her a polite wave.

Now that I'm at Liesel's house, Dee's smell is stronger. She's visited recently, and that might just be enough to get me to her. In the driveway, I pick up the tang of a different car—one that doesn't seem to belong to Liesel. It has a slight oil leak.

That should be enough. I bend down and sniff around the driveway, following the smell back into the street. I follow it to the closest intersection, where it curves around and continues to the right, along a larger road.

Now that I have the trail, it's much faster for me to follow it. My blood turns warm thinking about where this trail leads me, who might be waiting for me on the other end. It leads me through the city, and even though my legs are growing tired and the cement is hot under my paws, I keep going as her path leads me out of Aston.

It will take me some time to get back to my car, and I hope I make it to work on time.

The sun is low in the sky by the time I finally reach a suburban development with a few shops and a grocery store. The scent of Dee's car winds through the parking lot, and I dodge cars as I follow it. This is another human area, and people are surprised to see a wolfman running about like a loose dog. But I ignore them as the trail passes through the gas station and then back onto the street.

Finally, just when I think I might have to give up so I can get to work on time, the scent of her car approaches a cute duplex and stops in the two-car lot. On the upper floor is a balcony, with a few pots full of blossoming plants leaning over the railing.

The scent of Dee is all over it. But it's not fresh, and there are many other smells tangled up with it. She must not be here, and perhaps hasn't been all day.

At least now I know where she lives—that's the ideal first step. I got much farther than that worthless PI did. Now all I need to do is come back when she's home and knock on her front door.

Surely she felt the same thing I did, and she'll understand why I'm here. What happened between us... I'm positive that it wasn't one-sided. I hope Dee still thinks of me the way I fantasize about her.

Buoyed by this thought, I start the long journey back to Aston to get my car.

ten

DEE

INTRODUCING Boomer to his new home has been a challenge, but Robbie has quickly made himself invaluable.

"I love dogs," he explains. "I always had one growing up, but now, I don't want to leave one at home while I'm at work all day." He grins. "So maybe I can just, you know, borrow yours sometimes."

He gives me tips to stop Boomer from pulling on walks, and helps me install a bell on the door so eventually, the dog can tell me when he wants to go to the bathroom. I'm not sure how a dog could figure that out, but Robbie assures me that dogs are quick to learn.

Boomer, on the other hand, does not have much interest in learning. He simply stands at the door and gives a little whine when he wants to pee, so after a while we take the bell down. Then he takes his time sniffing the same spot he always loves to sniff, and I stand there enjoying the morning air until he's finally sniffed every last inch of it.

One Saturday afternoon, Robbie invites Boomer and I

over to enjoy some sunshine on the back patio. Robbie owns a townhome fairly close to my apartment, with a tiny backyard perfect for lounging and watching Boomer play with his new toy. He thrashes his head back and forth as it squeaks in his jaws, and it's possibly the cutest thing I've ever seen.

I do miss beer on days like today.

"You know, I never asked what you do for work," I say to fill the silence.

Robbie shrugs. "It's boring. I'm an account manager, and I handle some of our more high-priority clients and teach them how to use our software."

"Yeah, sounds boring," I agree. Robbie quirks his eyebrow at me, then turns back to Boomer.

"You've never explained what your job is," he says after a time. So we both know that I've been cagey about it. I've tried to avoid the question as long as I can, but now he's asking me point-blank.

"Well, uh..." Shit. I didn't want to have to tell him this soon. Maybe the sex wasn't mind-blowing, but he's an all right guy. Not the sort of person I see myself settling down with, but maybe that's because there's only one creature in the world with whom I could have ever seen that future.

Bill.

Which is insane, now that I think about it. All we did was fuck—twice. I don't even know what his face looks like. And I have to explain that to this guy I've just met?

"Is it something illegal?" Robbie asks at my silence. "Are you a criminal?"

I snort-laugh at this. "No, no. It's all above-board."

"'Above-board'?" he asks, bewildered. "Is there a chance that it could be below-board?"

I shrug helplessly. I guess I have to fess up now if I don't want him to think I'm a mobster.

"I'm, um..." I want to say, *A wolfman with a great dick bred me full of his cub.* Instead, the words that come out are: "I'm a surrogate."

Robbie blinks. "A surrogate? Like you bid for people at auctions?"

Now it's my turn to stare. "What? No. Like, uh, you know." I gesture downwards at my abdomen. "Like, babies?"

I can see the moment it clicks because his mouth falls open. He gapes at me as his eyes travel down to my flat stomach, then back up again.

"You're pregnant?" he asks. I think the best description for his face is *flabbergasted.* "Seriously? With... some random person's kid?"

I nod slowly. "Yep. That's my job. Incubating for the next... eight months now, I guess."

There's a quick flash of disgust on his face, but he quickly hides it. I suppose I should've expected that—and maybe I should have told him before he slept with me—but I can't take it back.

"Huh." He thinks it over for a long moment, and then his lips quirk up. "I didn't know that was a job."

I offer him a shrug. "Yep. People who can't have kids on their own hire me. It's through an agency, though, so it's all anonymous."

I thought that would make it better, but his eyes go wide. "So you don't even know the parents?"

I'm one of the parents, I want to say. But at the end of the day, I won't be. I'm more of an egg donor, if I'm being honest with myself.

"Nope," I finally tell him. "Really, it's just a job. It definitely pays better than my last one."

I can already tell Robbie looks at me differently now, which I expected. I guess if he asks me to leave, I know how better to go about the next relationship, if there is one. I'll just be up-front at the start.

After a few moments of thought, though, Robbie's eyebrows lower and his mouth curls on one side. "So, basically," he says, "you can't get pregnant again."

It catches me off-guard. "Well, uh, no. Generally that's how biology works."

"And you're going to carry it for the whole nine months?"

I'm about to correct him by saying *actually, it's ten*, but stop myself. The last thing I need is to add fuel to the fire and reveal that the father of my baby is a wolfman.

"That's the plan," I say cheerfully.

Robbie's rather wicked smile spreads further. "You know, it's always been kind of a... hm, fantasy of mine." He sets down his glass of orange juice and gets out of his chair. "To have sex with a pregnant woman."

My eyes must get as big as saucers when he says this, because Robbie's mouth closes and he stops moving towards me.

"Is that weird?" he asks. "I feel like that was weird."

"Hey, man," I say, raising both hands. "I'm not going to kink-shame you."

With an even bigger, almost ominous grin, he reaches the other side of the table and holds out his hand.

"Good. Then I have some things I'd like to do with you."

"All right." I accept it, because maybe it will ease my need for just another night. Robbie leads me to the back door of the house, and we go inside.

But as he gets on top of me and slips in his human cock, I can't keep my mind from wandering. He thrusts in and out, and I make the appropriate sounds, but I know that something is missing.

I wonder where Bill is tonight.

Is he fucking some lady wolf? Or even another human, like me? But I get the sense that if that were an option for him, he'd never have come to DreamTogether in the first place.

Perhaps it's cruel of me, but believing that he's alone lets me hope that maybe, just maybe, he's thinking about me, too. I don't want to imagine him with anyone else, or what his life might be like beyond our two brief dalliances.

I want him to be trapped in that moment in time so that he's still there someday, if I can find him again.

RUSS

When I get off work the next morning, I'm nearly dead on my feet. I desperately need some sleep—but first, I need to go by Dee's house and see if she's home yet.

I'm not going to go throw a rock at her window and ask her to come out on the balcony or anything. I just need to breathe in her fresh smell, and see that she got back safely from wherever she went today.

But when I pull up in front of the duplex, her car still isn't there, and when I get out and sniff the air, her scent is even fainter than before.

It unsettles my stomach. Where could she be that she was out all day and all night? My hackles raise, imagining what could have happened to her out there in the world. But I'm much too tired to try to track down her car, so I drive home and stumble my way up the stairs and into my bed, simply hoping that she's all right. I've never thought thirty-six was "old," but right now I certainly don't feel like a young cub anymore. My legs ache and my paws are almost raw on the bottom, but it was all worth it now that I know where to find Dee next time.

I'm up after only five hours of sleep, because my body knows that today is a day for action. I'll be reunited with her, and then finally, I can sleep soundly with my mate in my arms.

I make sure to clean up first, taking a long shower where I soap up all my fur, working my claws through it, and then I even spring for conditioner. When I'm silky soft from head to toe, including my tail, I rinse it all off and hop out of the shower. Then I shake, flinging droplets of water everywhere. There's a good reason my whole bathroom is tile with a drain in the middle.

I usually let myself air dry, but I need to get going, so I pull out the dryer and stand in front of it. But when I'm finished and peer at myself in the mirror, I'm horrified to see that my thick, brown fur is completely fluffy all over.

I can't deal with this right now. Grabbing a brush, I put some kind of hair product in it and run it through my fur, trying to push it back into place. Becoming presentable takes a good half hour, and even then, I look like a bow slapped on a pig.

This is not how I wanted our first meeting as our real selves to go.

I manage to brush my teeth and then I head out the door, just as it's starting to become late afternoon. When I finally make it to her place on the other side of Aston, it's almost sunset.

Her car is here this time, thankfully. Like before, I park around the corner. I want to be as unassuming as possible. I don't think she'll find me threatening—she did sign up to let me fuck her and then carry my cub—but I don't want to come on too strong, either.

Shit. I should've gotten flowers.

No, no. This is better. *That* would be coming on too strong. I'm dressed in a basic t-shirt and jeans, hoping to keep it casual. She seemed like the kind of woman who lives casually.

I feel like I know so much about her, and then also nothing at all. What if in real life, she's not like she was on the breeding bench? Will she be horrified to see my face, rather than just feeling me behind her?

This was such a bad idea.

But I'm too far in it now. If I have even a ghost of a chance at being with Dee, putting myself out there is completely worthwhile. Maybe she turns me down, but at least I'll get to see her up close, and know that she and my cub are safe here.

I'm about to step out into the street opposite her duplex when a car pulls up to the curb. A human man gets out, with brown hair that's been a little too manicured, and a scrawny build. Well, I guess any human has a scrawny build compared to me.

I retreat back onto the sidewalk as he heads to the duplex, goes up the stairs, and knocks. Then the door opens, and I see her.

Amanda. It's Dee, with long, dark hair pulled into a thick braid over her shoulder, and a face I'll never, ever forget.

She has wide blue eyes, so big it feels like they could

swallow me. Her forehead curves into an adorable nose, above a mouth with pouty lips. I couldn't imagine any creature more beautiful. Not even my fantasies compare to what she looks like in flesh and blood.

Dee doesn't spot me down on the sidewalk, so I scurry to the edge of the nearest house and step into the long, afternoon shadow. There, I watch as she leans forward, and the man standing at her door meets her halfway to kiss her on the lips.

The growl pours out of me before I can stop it. Both of them jerk, eyes darting around at the noise. I quickly duck around the corner toward my car, then climb in. I don't realize I'm panting until the windshield starts to fog up.

She has someone. Someone who isn't *me*.

My mind is ablaze with angry questions. Did she already have a partner when she let me fuck her full of my cub? Did I not have a chance to begin with? Or has she found this pathetic human man since her time with me?

Damn it. I squeeze the steering wheel tight. I fucked up by coming here. I should never have gone looking for her. I just didn't imagine that...

What? That she had an entire life that existed before me, and she would have another one after? That's an impossible ask. Her world doesn't revolve around me, a total stranger. It was meant to be anonymous.

And yet, every last one of my instincts is rioting, demanding that I go back to that house and tear that man apart, limb from limb. She is *mine*, and surely she knows it.

I shake my head rapidly and plop my forehead onto the steering wheel. I can't behave like that. I can't even have thoughts like that. But it would be impossibly cruel of the world to match me up with the perfect woman if I can't have her.

But that's not why I'm here. I curl my hand into a fist and breathe deeply. I'm here to keep anything from happening to her. I'm here to make sure no danger comes near her or my cub.

I don't have to be in her life to do it.

eleven

DEE

AT LEAST I'M not all alone anymore.

Robbie comes over a few times a week, and we go on walks with Boomer, cook dinner and fuck before we both pass out. I don't love that he sleeps over, but I'm learning to accept it as long as he stays on his side of the bed.

The guy's a lot softer than he seems at first, and likes having tender moments, which I do my best to reciprocate. I might even call him a little clingy with how often he texts and asks me out. Those are all qualities I should like in a partner, but it's just not doing it for me.

No, if I'm telling the truth, all I want is to get utterly ravaged by my wolfman. More often than not when we're in bed, that's what I think about, instead. I feel bad imagining something else when Robbie's inside me, and the feeling only gets worse the more time goes on.

I thought I'd forgotten about the stranger at DreamTogether by now, but I just can't seem to shake him.

At least the morning sickness has faded, but in its place

has emerged a new complication. Food I used to love doesn't taste as good as it once did, and I find myself lusting after things I'd never even considered delicious before. Robbie's confused when I decline the breadsticks at Olive Garden and order the fish.

"Didn't you say two weeks ago that you hate fish?" he asks, giving me a perplexed look.

"I don't know." I shrug. "It was just calling to me. I want that ocean smell."

He shakes his head. "Pregnant ladies. What'll it be next, haggis?"

I frown at him. It actually does sound good, but I definitely can't say that.

Almost every time I see him, I worry that I'm using Robbie just for his companionship, not because I really care or lust for him. But I also don't have the guts to tell him the truth, because in a way, he's all I have.

Well, and Boomer. When Robbie's not over, Boomer sits on the couch with me while I knit and watch television. We enjoy long walks, and often I bring a blanket to the park so we can sit together and watch people go by. I love his companionship, how easily he shows affection, how wonderful it is to show him affection in return. I have a timer set for his mealtimes, and I usually sneak a little bit of my dinner down to him, even though I know I shouldn't. Probably the only downside is that sometimes at night, he'll run to the sliding glass door that leads onto the balcony over the street and start barking like crazy, waking me up.

I don't know what it is that he sees out there, but I hope his vision isn't going bad. He's older for a dog his size, I know, and the last thing I want is for anything bad to happen to him so soon. I've grown pretty attached in a short period of time, and I think he has, too. He loves to climb up on my lap and lick my face, as if he were a much smaller dog, and parks himself at the foot of my bed every night to watch over me.

As much as I love my new apartment, though, and as well as my plants have taken to the new balcony, recently I've started feeling... unsettled. I can't put my finger on what it is, but it's like a tickle at the base of my neck I can't scratch away. I mostly feel it during the day, or late at night when Boomer wakes me up. Sometimes I think I see a black car following me when I do errands, and other times I notice strange shadows while I'm walking the dog.

Maybe pregnancy hormones are making me crazy. All sorts of other things have changed, so it wouldn't surprise me. And yet, as the weeks crawl by, I can't shake the sense that someone is watching me.

So I keep Boomer at my side at all times. I leave the lights on in the living room, even at night, to ward off anyone who might try to break in. Maybe I'm paranoid.

Life falls into a new pattern anyway, though, and I flow along with it. Once or twice a week I meet up with Liesel. Finally, I introduce her to Robbie, but as usual I can't read her at all. He's clearly unsettled by her, but puts on his game face because she's my best friend.

The next day, I call her up on the phone to get her opinion.

"Hmm," is all she says. "That's how I feel about him."

I shake my head in disbelief. "What does that mean?"

"He's fine. Nothing exciting, just fine."

When she says it, though, I think I know what she means. Robbie is a nice guy, and as my belly starts to show, he doesn't act like he minds. Still, he keeps a polite distance, never expressing affection or admiration for it.

And that's just fine with me. I'd rather pretend it wasn't

there, because these days, it only serves as a reminder I'll never see Bill again, and that sparks a drowning hopelessness in me.

"But do you want 'fine,' Dee?" Liesel asks, prying deeper. "Is that really going to satisfy you?"

I don't know how to explain to her that being with Robbie is not about being satisfied. It's about holding off the uglier thing hiding deep underneath it, the truth that I don't want to face.

"Find me a better option," I finally say. "I dare you. Who's going to date the lady whose job is to get pregnant?"

Liesel lets out a displeased *tsk*. "Just another McFlips," she says, but doesn't push me any farther.

I'm going to be content with what I have. Someday, I'll forget about him.

RUSS

It's agony, really. But I have no choice.

I watch my woman day in and day out. Whenever I'm not at work, I'm parked on various streets in her neighborhood, never returning to the same place too many times. The last thing I need is to arouse the suspicion of one of her neighbors.

After leaving my car, I find a comfortable spot where I can keep an eye on her house. I've got strong arms and big claws, so it's not too hard for me to climb up onto a roof nearby and observe from there. I learned early on not to get close to the house, because it appears Dee has a dog companion, and it diligently barks at me whenever it catches sight of me lurking around.

At least there's that. She has someone else watching over her, too, when I can't be around.

I follow her wherever she goes, whether it's to the grocery store, to Liesel's house, or to her boyfriend's place. Sometimes she drives a little erratically, which makes me crazy. I don't think I could bear her getting into a wreck. But I keep a few cars back, so that if such a thing were to happen, I would be there in a blink to help.

Every time she heads into Aston, I know she's on her way to see that fucking detestable man. When she parks in his driveway, I find a spot around the corner where my car is hidden from sight, and quietly close the door as I get out. I want to climb over the fence into his yard to get a better view, but Dee usually brings her dog with her, and it would go ballistic if it saw me.

I hate this human imposter. I fucking hate him more than I've ever hated anything. Whenever I see his face appear in a window I just want to punch him as hard as I can, so hard I knock him out or kill him.

Every so often at night, I hear her cry out, and I shudder all over knowing it's from someone else soaking in her hot, wet pussy. It should be me. My instincts almost boil over at the sound of it, and I have to tamp down the rabid urge to rush inside the house and tear them apart.

But her cries... aren't the same as what I remember. They're strange, almost false, and that gives me a faint glimmer of hope that maybe I still have a chance someday when she gets bored of her beau.

And that day will come, I know it. Then I'll make my move.

twelve

RUSS

MY FAVORITE ACTIVITY, which is, perhaps, also the most depressing one, is to sit in a high tree at the park and watch my Dee recline in the summer sunshine. Her water bottle rolls off to one side as she lies back, wrapping one arm around her dog and covering her eyes with the other. She's... perfect like this, her soft belly now gently swelled, visible even when she's flat on the ground. Sometimes she even lets out her long, dark hair, and more than once I've desperately wanted to jerk off in my hiding place up in the boughs.

Fuck, I need her. I need her like I've never needed anything, like food or water or sunshine.

But I can't ruin her life, either. She seems to be happy—or happy enough. If I did appear at her door as Bill, there's a very good chance she'd turn me away.

I don't think I could stand that.

It's a Tuesday when I'm watching Dee at the park before work, relishing how the sun plays off her skin, how she rests one hand on her stomach like she's protecting it. I shift in my position in the tree, trying not to make the branches creak. My legs are starting to fall asleep from standing crouched for so long, but I have to stay alert. Anything could happen out in the open like this.

On the path nearby, a runner goes past with a dog in tow. The dog isn't leashed, though, and the moment it sees Dee's sweet hound...

It takes a hard right turn and lunges towards them.

I'm on the ground before I even realize I've jumped out of the tree. Fueled by pure instinct, I sprint across the grass, toward the dog with the bared teeth. Dee still has no idea, and remains supine on her picnic blanket.

Thankfully, her own dog leaps to its feet and instantly jumps into action.

I come to a grinding halt as the two dogs start going at it. Dee jerks upright as growls and snarls fill the air, and she lets out a shrill cry. I hesitate, not sure if I should intervene or not and reveal myself. While my woman and my cub aren't directly at risk, I don't want anything to happen to her beloved companion, either.

"What the fuck?" Dee shouts, then dives at the two dogs. Shit. That's not good—someone as small and fragile as her shouldn't get in the middle of a dogfight. The runner is also rushing toward her pet, hand outstretched. This isn't going to go well.

My instincts know only one thing: keep Dee safe, even if it means she learns my secret.

One, two, three strides, and I have my arms wrapped around her, dragging her away from the fight. Then, once she's stunned and set on the ground safely a few feet away, I dive for the two dogs.

First I grab the attacker by the head, squeezing my fingers between its jaws to pull it off of Dee's pet. It yowls as I haul it backwards, and there's blood on my hands where it got its teeth into the other dog's flesh. Cursing, I hurl it to one side, and it rolls on the grass before springing back to its feet. I turn to face it, putting my body between the two animals, and it lunges again—this time, right at me.

It's easy to block with my arm, though, and the beast clamps its jaws around my wrist.

"Poppy! Stop!" the runner calls out, and I realize that she and Dee have both been screaming for some time. "Poppy!" I'm bleeding now, too, but there's not much the dog's jaws can do against my thick fur and skin. The runner grabs her dog by the collar, tears streaming down her face as she tugs on it, trying to get it to release me. "I'm sorry, I'm so sorry!"

Slowly I lower the dog to the ground while it snarls and wriggles, then I pry its jaws off of me. Once I'm freed, the woman snaps her leash onto the dog's collar and starts dragging it away.

"Keep your damned animal under control," I snap at her, and her eyes grow huge. Then I spin around to check the damage.

I find Dee on her knees next to her dog, who's whimpering pathetically. I kneel down beside her, where she sits sobbing.

"Boomer!" She's petting him, clearly in shock. "Are you okay, buddy? Oh, look at your ear!" I want to pat her back and assure her that he'll be all right, but she might not welcome it. Instead, I pull out my phone and start to dial 9-1-1.

"I'll call someone," I say. But Dee quickly stops me with a hand on my arm. My hackles raise, highly aware of her touch, and I almost pull away because the shock of it is so powerful.

"Don't," she says, glaring at the jogger who's still standing there, watching us. "I'll handle it." Suddenly her voice is firm, despite the shakiness from her tears. Dee pulls out her own phone and stalks toward the woman with the other dog. "Give me your number, your name, and your address."

The runner holds her dog tight as it snarls, and lists off all the information. When they're finished, the jogger leaves, dragging her animal along behind her.

Dee looks something up on her phone, then dials. "Hello? My dog was just attacked, and I need someone to look at him." She pauses for a second. "Okay, you have a spot now? I'll be right there." She turns off the phone, shoves it in her pocket, and sprints back over to us.

"Are you taking him to the vet?" I ask as the brown dog paws at his torn ear.

"Yeah, right now. Thanks for your help, wolfman." She takes the leash in her hand and offers me a thin half-smile— until her eyes travel down to my arm, where blood is dripping through my fur. Her mouth falls open in horror.

"Oh, fuck," she says, grabbing my arm to get a better look. Her tears start coming again. "Please, please don't sue me."

I frown at her. "Sue you? Why would I sue you?" I jerk a thumb in the direction the runner went. "I should be suing her."

"Please don't sue anyone." She helps her dog to his feet and starts walking away, but then stops and gestures for me to follow. Obediently, I do.

"Come on," she says. "I'll take you to the hospital right after we drop Boomer off at the vet. He'll probably need stitches."

I arch an eyebrow at her. "Vet first?" I ask, in a joking tone. "I know where I fall on the food chain."

Despite her tears, Dee smiles. "Sorry. He's just... he

means a lot to me." The dog is still letting out pathetic sounds as she winds through the park toward the exit.

"I understand," I say, even though I've never had a pet myself. Dee tilts her head at me as we walk, and she squints.

"Do I know you from somewhere?" she asks. "Your voice sounds familiar."

I try not to show how this makes me feel: giddy and pleased. So she remembers me that well, does she?

But I shake my head. "I don't think so," I say, fishing for something that might throw her off the scent. "Though I've been told there's a radio DJ who sounds like me."

"That must be it." Dee shrugs then resumes leading me to her car. I already know which one it is, and head toward it to open the door. She stops cold.

"How did you know that one was mine?" she asks, pointedly peering down the row of other cars parallel parked there.

"Well, uh," I search for something to say that won't give me away. "You were headed right to this one. I thought I'd try to help."

She inspects me for a moment, then nods and allows me to open the back door of her sedan. As she helps Boomer up into the seat, I go around to the passenger side, even though my own car is quite close by and I could easily drive myself to the hospital.

Not that I need a hospital. It isn't as serious as it looks, but if I get to spend even a few moments with Dee, breathing in her smell, I'll die happy.

I awkwardly wedge myself into the little human-made car, and Dee gawps at me. "Oh, gosh, sorry. I forgot that you're huge. And you might not fit."

I curl my shoulders and lower my head so I don't bump the roof, then smile at her. "It's fine. Thanks for taking me."

"Sure. I'm sorry again about what happened." She starts up the old car and it coughs.

"You didn't do anything wrong." I want nothing more than to reach out and touch her, to assure her that I'm fine and I would do anything to take care of her and my cub, but I keep my hand pressed down in my lap. "I saw a woman in need, and so I stepped in. That's all."

She gives me a wan smile. "I'm glad you did. I think Boomer would be a lot more injured right now if you hadn't."

This is probably true. My heart is still racing at how close she and my cub came to danger, and I'm immensely grateful I was there.

Then we're off. We wind through town, Dee remaining quiet. Suddenly, though, she turns to me and asks, "Wait, what's your name? I never got your name."

I chuckle. "Russ."

"What were you doing at the park? Going on a walk?"

"Yeah," I lie. "Enjoying the sunshine before I have to go to work. I live close by."

She hums thoughtfully as she makes her way into the parking lot of a strip mall. "Well, I'm glad you were there. Russ."

Holy shit, my name sounds good on her tongue. A shiver crawls along every inch of my body, rippling my fur.

Dee blinks. "You okay?"

"Oh, yeah, fine." As she gets out of the car, I push my own door open to follow her. "Here, I should come with you. In case they ask questions."

Dee tilts her head, then nods and opens the back door to let out Boomer. The sweet dog is still whimpering as she leads him inside the vet's office, and I think he might be hamming it up for her. Dee eats it up, crooning, "My poor baby," and petting his head as they walk.

I stand next to her as we wait behind someone at the counter, and my nostrils are full with the delicious scent of her. I could just eat her up right here, push her against a wall and fuck her like—

I cut myself off and shake my head to clear it. I'm only here to support her right now, that's all. Her best friend in the world was just mauled. As we step up to the counter and Dee starts talking to the receptionist, though, an idea strikes me.

Maybe that's the answer to all this. *Be like Boomer.* I can't tell her what she means to me, how desperately I need her and her cub under my care. She already has someone, and I'd risk her shutting me out completely.

No, instead of announcing to her that I'm Bill... I'll be there for her. I'll become her friend, and get her to trust me.

And then I'll convince her to fall in love with me.

thirteen

DEE

BOOMER IS GOING to be all right, the vet tells me. He won't even need stitches or anything like that. The blood just makes it look worse than it is.

"I'm not a doctor," the vet says when Russ tells her his story, "but let me take a look at that bite of yours." She shaves away some of his fur, then cleans off the blood. "Oh, that's not too bad. Much better than it looks."

I let out a relieved breath of air. Thank goodness. I really didn't want to have to take on the wolfman's medical bills, when I certainly would out of guilt.

"Guess I don't need to visit the hospital," he says as the vet applies ointment and then bandages up the wound. He's being a really great sport about this.

"That's good. Then I can drop you off and take Boomer back home."

We say goodbye to the vet, and Boomer seems to be in a much better mood as we leave. That's probably because of the ten treats we gave him while we were waiting.

The wolfman tilts his head down to me. "Are you sure you're going to be okay alone?"

Immediately, I want to say, *no, I don't want to be alone. Please come home with me, you complete stranger.* Because fuck, when he picked me up and moved me out of the path of danger, then intervened in the fight...

I thought of Bill. And every moment since then I've been thinking of Bill, and for a split second I even wondered if fucking a different wolfman would sate my need.

I blame the drama today. It was a lot to take in, and my heart is still beating a million miles a minute. I'm not thinking straight at all. This guy hasn't expressed a lick of interest in me, just gone along for the ride as I've whirl-winded him off.

Or, maybe his question is an invitation.

"I think I'll be all right on my own," I finally answer. "They gave me some pain meds for Boomer, and my—"

I cut myself off. Do I want to tell this guy I have a boyfriend? It's kind of sick of me not to say it right away, to make it clear I'm not available. It's unkind to Robbie, at least, who's not a bad guy by any stretch. He doesn't deserve for me to hide him.

And yet I say, "My friend will be over later tonight anyway, because we had a hang-out planned."

"Do you need company until then?" Russ asks as I help Boomer up into the seat.

I peer at him over the top of my car, which he dwarfs rather comically. Is he hitting on me? Or just being kind?

"Um," I begin, unsure of what's safe and what isn't. If I do get him alone in my house, and he *is* hitting on me... Again I think of Bill, and how fucking delicious he felt inside me, and Russ blinks, tilting his head.

"You all right?" When I still don't answer immediately,

because I don't know what to say, he taps the top of the car. "It's decided. I'll come with you to take Boomer home, and then we're getting iced coffees. You look like you've seen a ghost and I think you need to relax and come down."

Eventually, I nod in agreement. "Yeah, you're probably right," I say, because my hands are still trembling. "I feel like I'm finally realizing what happened."

"Yeah, it's called shock." Russ climbs back in the passenger seat, curling his shoulders to fit inside my little vehicle. As I put the car into drive, I wonder if I'm making a huge mistake.

But as I pull out into the street, it's not one I want to correct. Maybe he isn't Bill, but something about him makes me feel... safe. Protected.

Probably because he literally just saved and protected you, I think to myself. But right now that's what I need.

Russ the wolfman is, though, rather polite. When we get back to my place, he waits in the driveway with the car while I get Boomer set up on the couch. My dog happily accepts, and seems to have fully recovered from his run-in already, so I kiss him on the nose before locking the door behind me.

To my surprise, Russ knows the area pretty well, and guides me to a cute little coffee shop I haven't seen before.

"This area's still new to me," I tell him as we park. "I haven't lived here long, so I'm happy to learn about all the neat little hole-in-the-wall places."

It is odd that he knows so much about a predominantly human area, but he did say he lives close by. Maybe he's a bouncer, or an armored guard. Lots of humans hire out monsters for work that requires someone big and scary.

Inside, Russ keeps his hands in his pockets, then summons me to order my drink.

"I can buy it—" I begin.

"You're the one who's in shock. Please tell the man your order."

The way he gently bosses me around instantly turns me on. I can almost hear Bill's gravelly voice telling me what to do and how he's going to fuck me.

All I have to do is *think* about him and I'm already getting wet.

Russ's eyebrows go up as we stand waiting for our orders. He glances at me from the side of his eye, then turns back to waiting. Once we have our drinks, we head for a table outside.

"Thanks again," I say as we sit down. "For saving my bacon and Boomer's, and then treating me to coffee."

He leans down and laps up his drink. I don't know why I didn't expect that, that he would drink like... well, a wolf. Then he lifts his head again and studies me.

"It's really not a problem," he says, and his voice is softer. "You don't have to thank me for doing the decent thing."

I'm about to argue, but then I try to take his point to heart. He's a good guy, and he was just doing as duty called on him.

In a way, though, that kills my buzz. It wasn't because of some hidden crush on me that he stepped in to help. He did it because it was right.

I gesture at his arm. "At least that should heal fast, like the vet said." I giggle at the square of shaved fur around the wound. His skin is a pinkish-brown under his tawny pelt. "Sorry about that, though."

He shrugs. "I'll wear it to work with pride." Then, suddenly, his eyes get huge. "Oh, fuck." He glances down at his watch, then shoots me another panicked look. "I need to go. I'm so sorry."

"Are you late?" I jump out of my chair and grab my coffee. "Come on, I'll take you back to your house."

Russ waves his hands. "No, no, it's fine. I'll just call a cab from here, it'll be faster." He takes out his phone and presses the screen a few times, and I'm surprised his claws don't get in the way.

"How far are you going? I could take you."

He glances at me, an uncertain look on his face. Maybe I'm taking this too far by even suggesting it? I'm about to rescind my offer when he nods briefly.

"Okay. Sure. I work at the hospital in Dunsville."

I blink. "You work in Dunsville but live here?" It's a good thirty minutes.

"I understand if you don't want to drive that far," he says apologetically. "Just let me call for a ride, and—"

"No, no," I say, waving my hands. "Come on. If it's not too uncomfortable in my car."

He shakes his head vigorously. "I would love that. Thank you."

This time when we get in, I remember that I have an ancient sunroof. When I open it, he tilts his head and breathes in a big whiff of the passing air.

Damn. This should probably be the last time I see this guy if I don't want to catapult head-over-heels for him.

RUSS

I don't have half the things I need for a night at the hospital, but I'll survive with what's in my office. I always keep an extra set of scrubs and shoes in the closet, just in case. There's no way I'd pass up the chance to sit in the car with Dee for half an hour, even if it gives me a massive crick in my neck and a raging boner. I keep my injured arm carefully placed over it, in case she glances away from the road.

Her scent spiked while we were waiting for our coffee, and I'm still wondering what she was thinking about. Is it too much to hope that it was me?

Ugh. It was probably her boyfriend. She hasn't told me about him yet, and I'm not sure how I should act when she tells me. *If* she tells me.

If she doesn't... I could interpret that message, but I don't want to hope yet.

When I give her the hospital address, she raises an eyebrow. "So what do you do at the hospital?"

"I'm a doctor. I work in the maternity ward."

Her mouth bobs open, and then she quickly rights it and turns the car on.

"Wow. So you deliver babies?"

"Lots of them," I say, a little pride in my voice.

But instead of answering, Dee falls silent, and she's staring ahead at the road with a puzzled look on her face.

"Is that odd?" I ask. "A guy who delivers babies?"

She flashes me a panicked look. "No, no, not at all. It's... it's nice. I guess." She twists up her mouth like she wanted to say something else. "It's really good, yeah. I just, um..."

"You can say what you're thinking," I tell her gently. "I'm not going to judge you for it."

A smile curls her lips. "Well, uh, it's just interesting you say that, because I'm pregnant."

I bite my lip to keep from saying, *I know*. Instead, I offer her a radiant smile. "Congratulations. That's wonderful news."

She nods, but then her smile falls. "But it's a weird situation," she goes on.

"How is it weird?" I ask. "It's amazing, what your body can do."

This stuns her, and she turns her gaze away from the road to give me an unguarded smile. "Yeah, I guess it is," she says as she turns back to her driving, much to my relief. "But it's not my baby."

I cringe. So that's how she sees it. She's not carrying *our* cub, she's carrying *mine*. At least, in her mind.

"Oh?" I ask instead, trying to sound surprised rather than displeased. "You're right, that is an unusual situation."

I leave it there, hoping the door is open enough in case she wants to tell me more. I'd love to be that for her, someone she can talk to, and be honest with.

"I guess I don't need to tell you my whole life story." She gives a melancholy laugh.

"I want to hear whatever you'll tell me."

Dee glances at me from the corner of her eye. "You're a cool guy, Russ," she says. "But I don't know if you would really understand."

I give her a playful smirk. "Try me."

With a deep inhale, she seems to decide to trust me, and starts talking.

"I did this program where... um..." Her face is already turning a cute pinkish-red. "...where I carry a monster's baby. And it was, uh, a wolfman. Who picked me."

She purses her lips together, like she already regrets

saying it. I make sure to look appropriately amazed, but not horrified or judgmental.

"I haven't heard of a program like that," I say, falling easily into the lie. Shit. This would be the moment to say, *Oh, DreamTogether? I did that, too. I wonder if I was that wolfman. Have you ever met Bill?* But the words have already come out.

Besides, I don't want to risk damaging this fragile thing between us, between the real Dee and the real Russ.

"And so that's how you got pregnant?" I say instead. "Another wolfman, like me?"

I don't mean it to come out almost... sultry, but I can't help it. The smell in the car has changed, and I know exactly what it is.

She's reacting to me, her body recognizing me.

"Yup," she says, then abruptly falls silent again. I'm not sure what I did, but whatever it was, it stopped the conversation quickly.

After a while, I reach down to play with the radio.

"It doesn't work," Dee says. "Sorry."

Soon we're on the highway, and I wish I knew what I'd said to make her clam up. She's fixated on the road, brow furrowed in concentration. Before long we've reached the hospital.

"Hey," Dee says as I reach for the door handle. She takes a deep breath, and the creases in her face fade into a worn-out smile. "Thank you again. I know you asked me not to say that, but I'm going to say it anyway. You seriously saved us today. Especially Boomer." She smiles. "Unfortunately, I have a boyfriend, or else I'd ask you to get coffee with me again. I really enjoyed getting to know you, Russ."

I hover over the handle, then let it go and turn to face her.

"You're going it alone," I say. "Aren't you?"

She frowns. "Well, I sort of have Robbie..."

"Right." I should stop now, before I make an ass of myself. "But you're going to go through a lot of changes, a lot of difficult moments, and I hope you have a support network around you to help you through it."

When Dee blinks those huge blue eyes at me, I just want to ravage her. I want to lick her and stuff her full of me and fall asleep curled up around her. I want to hold her forever, to love her and support her through all of this.

"If you ever need someone to talk to, someone with a *little* bit of experience in the field..." I grin, trying not to show too many of my teeth, "then please call me." I open my wallet and fish a card out of it, then pass it to her. She looks down at it, and then back up at me with moisture on her lashes.

"Oh. Thank you." I wonder if I've hurt her in some way, but then she smiles through her brimming tears. "I do feel... alone, sometimes. Maybe we could have coffee, then. Just as friends."

I beam at her. "I would love that. I need an update on Boomer, anyway." I finally open the door of the car and step into the sunshine, stretching now that I can stand up straight.

"Thanks again, Russ," Dee calls out the window as I head to the front doors, already terribly late.

"You're welcome." She gets a big grin on her face before she pulls away, and I feel like I could fly.

fourteen

DEE

I CAN'T STOP THINKING about Russ all night. In fact, I call Robbie and tell him I'm not feeling that great after the attack today, and though he's concerned about Boomer, he agrees to meet up with me tomorrow, instead.

I hate that he asks if I need anything. The way I've already fantasized about wolfman cock tonight, it's not fair to him. But I tell him we're both all right, and we had some help along the way.

That night I pull out the dilator that DreamTogether gave me, and use it on myself. This time I'm thinking about Bill, and then about Russ, and the two blend together in my imagination.

They do have similar voices, if I remember Bill's right. But Russ had no clue what I was talking about when I mentioned DreamTogether, and maybe I don't know him that well, but it seemed like genuine surprise.

I mean, there's more than one wolfman in the tri-county area. Of course he's not the same guy.

But damn, do I wish. Do I wish more than anything that Bill would magically reappear. That he would find me, somehow, amidst all this chaos that is civilization, and make me his in real life, too.

I wonder how much he and Russ look alike. Does Bill have those same deep, amber eyes? I imagine Russ pushing me down on the bed, caging me in with his huge body. It's easy to remember how Bill lavished attention on me, licking me everywhere, shoving his tongue inside me and fucking me with it until I squirted into his waiting mouth.

Oh, and then his cock. While my pussy was still swollen, he would slide it into me slowly, the way he did at DreamTogether. He would let me adjust to him before he really let me have it, burying himself deep and then yanking out in a steady, perfect rhythm.

Not to mention that knot. Fuck, I could never forget how Bill had worked it inside me, lathering me up and softening me until it fit through. Nothing again could compare to the way he plunged it in, over and over, then pulled it free again. And once he got it all the way through...

I orgasm thinking of him coming inside me, filling me up with his warm seed, which then found its way deep into my womb.

Surely Russ would have a knot, too. I wonder if he would feel just as good.

When I've cleaned up, I pull out my phone and the business card Russ gave me, and draft a text message. I feel bad about how I reacted in the car today, how I shut down when I realized just how attractive he was and how much it stirred up in me.

> Hi, Russ, it's Dee. I just wanted to give you my phone number so you have it.

A few moments pass, and then I see three dots appear.

> Nice to hear from you, Dee. I'm glad to have your number now. Are you feeling better?

I smile down at my phone. He's so polite, and yet I can already tell he has a hidden, dominant side to him.

> Yeah, much better.

> How was visiting with your friend?

Fuck. I forgot that I'd lied about that.

> It was nice to see her.

> Good. Reach out to me anytime you need to talk.

I heart his message, and I begin writing something back when I stop myself.

I have a boyfriend, like I told him, and I shouldn't cross the line. So I leave it that way and crawl back onto the couch with Boomer to finish watching our movie.

But when I'm in my bed that night, I imagine Russ's long snout, his intense, yellow eyes, and his big, clawed hands. I imagine him fucking me the way Bill did, and it's easy to meet my climax again.

RUSS

The days of waiting are agonizing.

I'm patiently allowing Dee to come to me first, giving her room to sort through things. Maybe she won't call on me after all, deciding what I'm offering hovers too close to the edge of platonic—though I tried my best in my texts to keep it light and friendly.

That doesn't mean I don't continue my watch. Already I've managed to protect her and our cub once, and I will do it again in a heartbeat, should I need to. But then the days turn into a week, and it's crushing my soul knowing that I have her phone number, right there, and I could call her at any time. But I don't want to come on too strong and then push her away.

But after two weeks, I can't bear it any longer. Even if it's just pixels on a screen, I need to talk to her.

I know that she's often with her friend Liesel or her boyfriend in the evenings, so I choose midday to send her a message.

> I hope you and the cub are well. Make sure
> you're getting enough vitamins.

It's not a direct ask for a response, but one would be nice.

I watch through the window as she rises up from her couch. I can see inside through the sliding glass doors that lead onto her balcony, which affords me a view at her television over the back of the couch and part of her kitchen.

Dee paces back and forth in front of the glass, clearly looking down at the phone in her hand like she's trying to decide what to say.

I wonder what makes one innocuous message so fraught for her.

> Hey Russ. Thanks for reaching out. I'm sorry I haven't called. The nausea has mostly gone away, but now I feel achey all over.

I sympathize with this—it's a common complaint we get from expectant parents. I quickly type out a reply.

> We use topical muscle relaxant at the hospital. I can get some for you, if you'd like.

She pauses in front of the doors, then leans against her couch. I wish I could make out her facial expression as she writes out her answer.

> Thank you. I would really appreciate that. Can I treat you to coffee this time?

I wait a moment before answering so I don't seem too eager.

> Sure, sounds good. I'll meet you at the place we went last time, tomorrow at noon?

She flips over the couch, and for a moment I think she's hurt herself. I jump to my feet, but then I see her heels kick in the air.

> Great. See you then.

I think this is a good sign.

Like I promised, I pilfer some of the muscle relaxant at work that night, and come prepared with it to the coffee shop the next morning. I park beside Dee's little white sedan and shake my head, thinking how I might go about getting her a new, safer car.

If she were mine, I would make sure she had a vehicle with a perfect safety rating.

Inside the coffee shop, I find Dee waiting at one of the tables by the door. She hops out of her chair and smiles a wide smile when she sees me.

She lights up the whole damn room with that smile.

"Russ," she says, and the sound of my name coming out of her mouth absolutely electrifies me. "I'm happy to see you again."

I try not to admire her too obviously as she saunters up to the counter, but seeing her from behind like this, it's easy to picture her like she was on the bench, her ass bare and up in the air, her pink cunt shining for me.

When I take her again, which I will, I want to take her that way.

I order my drink, and Dee shoots me a look when I reach for my wallet. I hold my hands up in surrender as she whips out her card and pays for our drinks.

"It's that 'carrying a wolfman's baby' money," she says quietly, and a laugh bursts out of me. I'm glad she feels like it's hers, and I'm ecstatic that she's comfortable enough with me to make a joke.

We take a seat nearby, and I bring out the reusable tote bag where I stashed the cream. Then I slide it across the table like we're doing a drug deal.

"Don't tell anyone I brought you this," I say conspiratorially, and Dee giggles.

"I won't, I won't." She sticks it into her purse and snaps the top closed, glancing around like we're being watched. "Thank you. That was really nice of you."

"No problem. The aches and pains are normal. Be sure to use a heating pad on muscles that—"

"Yeah, yeah," she says, waving me off. "I know all about the heating pads. This ache feels deeper, though, like it's in my bones." She lets out a defeated sigh. "Is it going to be like this the whole time?"

A sadness washes over me. I know it's often an unpleasant thing to carry a child, but when I see parents together, often I see such joy, too. I wish I could share that with her, and be there every night to soothe away her aches and make her see stars, instead.

"No," I answer at last. "It won't always be like this. You'll find moments of happiness, too. You're doing something amazing." I lean forward on the table to lap up my drink. "It'll be worth it."

Dee nods slowly, then smiles up at me. It's a fake smile, a forced one, but I return it anyway. "Thanks for the words of wisdom," she says.

I try to veer the conversation away, somewhere safer where I can put my best foot forward as "platonic friend." I even inquire a little about her boyfriend, but she hesitates before talking about him.

"He's a good guy," is all she says. "Does some kind of computer thing." Then our conversation turns to Boomer and how well he's recovered since the attack, and Dee brightens up as she tells me he's good as new, minus a scar on his ear.

Eventually, the late morning becomes lunchtime, and she sighs over her empty iced coffee cup.

"Thanks for going out with me," Dee says. "I needed to leave the house."

"I'm happy to do it anytime. I don't usually work until the evening."

"You work night shift?" she asks. "That's rough."

"When you're a resident, you get used to it. And then I never really left." I don't tell her that I'm taking the night shifts because it pays better and I need the money for future childcare.

When we're finally at our cars and it's time to leave, Dee hesitates at her door.

"I'd like to do this again," she says, almost shyly. "I don't have a ton of friends, and definitely none who really understand what I'm going through."

I sure haven't spent much time with my own friends since I started my diligent watch over her, but I nod along.

"I'd be happy to," I say. "You have my number."

With that, we each get into our respective vehicles and wave goodbye.

Today feels like a good step. Now I understand better how she feels about her boyfriend, and I certainly wouldn't call it *passionate*. But I hate that she hurts, and carrying my cub is so physically and mentally draining for her. I'm nearly overwhelmed by the need to go after her as she drives away, to tell her that I'm Bill, that I'd care much better for her and our cub than that pathetic human man.

But I need her to trust me as Russ, to like me as Russ, to decide that Russ is a better fit for her.

Maybe soon, the next step will come.

DEE

The things that wolfman makes me feel should be considered criminal.

Just standing near him at the coffee shop, fuck. It was difficult to keep my hands to myself. I just wanted to run my fingers through his soft fur. His t-shirt complemented his broad chest perfectly, and he even had a pair of prominent pectoral muscles straining the fabric. His jeans were tight, showing off his ass while still leaving a slot for his big, fluffy tail. And his high ankles with the huge paws?

I can almost hear Bill's claws scraping the floor as he fucked me hard.

When Robbie comes over that night, I'm awash in guilt. I know I should break it off with him. We exchange a kiss when he comes inside, but I feel nothing behind it. He's become more like a friend, someone I can trust and rely on —but I find I lack any attraction. Especially now that I've met Russ, I can't say that the prospect of any human really draws me.

Robbie glances around my apartment as he sets down a bag of groceries. I've become a decent enough cook in the last few months, trying to meet the nutritional needs that DreamTogether has set out for me, and I'm planning to try a new recipe from my book tonight.

"Have you ever thought about getting a maid?" he asks, unpacking the bag. I frown, then pick a few stray objects off the counter to put them away.

"I can clean just fine myself," I say, a tad affronted by the way he's judging my lifestyle. I'm a little messy, sure, but it's not that bad. Maybe not as clean as Robbie is, but he keeps his home unnaturally clean and polished. I'll never be like that.

"There's dirty laundry all over your couch," Robbie points out. "Do you want me to work on that while you do dinner?"

As much as I don't like the idea of him dealing with my dirty clothes, if he wants to do it... I guess I won't stop him.

"Sure." He gathers up the clothes while I start chopping, and hustles off to the laundry machine. I should be grateful, I suppose, that he comes over and helps me out—but it feels almost hostile, like I'm not living up to his expectations for me.

With the machine going, he returns to the kitchen while I get the vegetables steaming. He runs a hand across my hip and down my ass, peering over my shoulder at what I'm cooking.

"Steamed again?" he asks, a trace of disappointment in his voice.

"I'm seasoning it after," I say defensively.

"Hmm." Robbie sits at the table and waits while I finish cooking. He pours himself a glass of wine from the bottle he keeps in the house, and I look on it with envy while he sips over dinner. He can do what he wants, of course, but sometimes I wish he wouldn't do it in front of me, at my house.

He doesn't say anything about the meal while we eat. I want to ask him if he likes it, but I find I don't care that much.

While he cleans up, the laundry machine goes off, and I go swap the clothes over to the dryer. When I get back, Robbie's cleaning more than just the dishes—he's scrubbing the counters and the cupboards, too. I find myself surprisingly insulted. It's not like the counters were all that dirty.

"What are you doing?" I ask.

"I just thought I'd help while I had the chance," Robbie

says, but I know it's not just that. It's judgment, an implication that I can't take care of myself.

"Well, you don't have to." As I put everything away, he looks rather irritated.

"If you move in with me, though, you'll need to be a lot cleaner."

I balk. "Who said anything about moving in together?"

He blinks at me like the thought of me refusing never even occurred to him. "Well, we see each other every other night. I thought it might be easier if you left this little apartment and moved in with me at my townhouse."

Fuck. Neither of us has dropped the "L" word yet, but I've gotten the sense recently that it's coming. Robbie's much deeper in this than I am, and has even hinted at meeting his parents.

"I like my apartment," I say defensively. "I'm not planning on going anywhere."

It looks like I've slapped him. "Oh. I thought that would be, you know, the end point of this."

"Well, it's not."

He's quieter after that as we sit down to watch a movie. That night, I have to focus hard to orgasm while he's on top of me. Afterwards, I head to the bathroom to pee and clean up, and when I get back, he's passed out cold.

Part of me, the selfish part of me, wants to hold onto Robbie until I find out whether Russ is an option. And that feels cruel and unfair, but so does breaking up with him when I know it would inevitably hurt him.

That's probably the biggest reason I should stop this now. If I care about Robbie, I should end it before he gets too deep. And yet, the prospect of being alone again feels even bigger and uglier than that.

Maybe I don't have to be alone though. I've never even

asked Russ if he's single, because at our level, it doesn't feel appropriate. He's made it clear that he'd like to be friends, but hasn't indicated anything else. It makes him feel both safe... and dangerous. I could see myself falling hard for him, but it might not be reciprocated.

I should probably never have invited Russ out with me, but damn if that cream doesn't work wonders. My aches don't keep me up late that night like they have for the last week, and I sleep like the dead.

The next morning, as Robbie gets dressed for work, he stops at the front door.

"I know you're going out at night a lot since you've had insomnia," he says. "But don't walk alone, okay? I don't want to worry about you when I'm not here."

I grumble something in agreement, but it's not like he can stop me. And I have Boomer.

Around lunchtime, I pull out my phone and hover over Russ's contact card. I should delete this. The longer we stay "friends," the more I'll become interested in him. Maybe I should introduce him to Robbie, and propose we all hang out. That would assuage my fears about going over the line, right?

Who the fuck am I kidding? I want to climb Russ Cohen like a tree.

And yet, that's only because of Bill. So here I am, holding onto Robbie because I crave company, and then holding onto Russ because I crave Bill—just using other people left and right.

Man, I'm a shitty person. A selfish, shitty person who

can't seem to get over a stranger I met twice, and I never even saw his face.

I take out my phone and type a message.

> Thank you for the cream, it helped immensely. But I probably shouldn't see you again. I'm sorry, Russ. I really enjoyed getting to know you.

I hover over the arrow that would send it. Can it still be considered a break-up text if we were never dating? That would be the end of whatever this is, and it won't go any further.

But what if there *could* be something there? I quickly delete the message, then smoosh my face into my throw pillow and wriggle on the couch. I don't want to utterly destroy something when I don't even know what it means yet.

The *whirr* of my robo-vacuum starts up, signaling the beginning of its scheduled, late-night trip around the house. I bought it to try to assuage Robbie, and now I simply watch it traverse the room, picking up one dust bunny after another while the television plays an infomercial.

Boomer gets up and nudges me, looking for a pat. He's not a big fan of our new friend. "Good boy," I tell him, scratching him behind the ears but avoiding the wound. "You always know when I need you."

Maybe I can divorce my libido from my interest in Russ. Maybe I can get to know him, on this platonic level, and see if what I feel for him is because of Bill, or because of *him*.

Still, strangely, it feels like cheating on Bill to even consider another wolfman. That's the most irrational thought in all this, and yet I still can't stop thinking about him.

Hoping for him.
Waiting for him.

fifteen

DEE

I GO a few more weeks without hearing from Russ. I know he's waiting for me to reach out, and I appreciate that about him. And how I want to, but it doesn't feel right. Whenever I get the urge, I go on a long walk with Boomer, or find a new, more complicated knitting pattern to try.

But sometimes when I'm up at night with my fresh case of insomnia, I sit in front of the TV, absently stroking my belly, and think about texting him, maybe even asking him to get coffee again. I know he would be up because he works the late shift. He might also be wrist-deep in a C-section.

Boomer crawls up onto the couch and lies down on my legs, his favorite spot. I got him a nice, fluffy bed on the floor, but he barely touches it. Right when I'm about to doze off to an old episode of *Contact List*, my phone buzzes.

It's Russ, as if he could read my mind. I eagerly open the message.

> How are you and the cub? I hope you don't mind me checking up, but I don't want you to feel alone in this.

My eyes well up immediately. They weren't kidding when they said pregnancy hormones make you emotional, because I also cried like a newborn at the ending to a movie about dinosaurs. But it's such a sweet gesture that it makes me warm knowing someone is thinking about my emotional health. Robbie's nice to me, but I wouldn't call him *attentive*, and he avoids touching my belly now when we have sex.

I think that Russ would take me and the baby as a package deal.

> Thanks for the thought.

I wipe the tears away from my eyes.

> It's nice, actually.

> I thought you might need a friend now.

For a moment, I almost wonder if he can see into my living room. Or maybe right into my brain? It's like he knew exactly when I could use a helping hand.

> Yeah, I do. Can't sleep. When I do sleep, I sleep all day.

There's a brief pause, and then the three dots appear.

> That happens sometimes. Your body is working hard and your rhythms are out of whack. The best thing you can do is not guilt yourself for it.

No advice about things I could do to help me sleep, suggestions which everyone and their mother seems to have. I've already tried them all, and none of them have worked.

Instead, he gave me an emotional tool, something I can actually use.

> Thank you. That... is really helpful.

> I'm glad. Anytime.

I bite my lip, trying to hold myself back from asking him to go out for coffee again. No, if I do that... I have to end it with Robbie, first.

> I really appreciate you messaging me. I hope you have a good night.

That's safe enough. He replies right away.

> You, too.

I heart his message, then lie back down on the couch, clutching my phone to my chest.

RUSS

I have been worried about her, seeing how late she keeps her lights on. That's why I messaged her, knowing she was awake.

Actually, I worry about her endlessly now, more and more every day. It haunts me when I'm asleep, thinking about where she is and what might happen to her while I'm not there to watch over her. It makes the long hours at work agonizing, imagining what dangers she might face out there in the world.

Of course I wish I wasn't like this. I wish that my kind had marriage bonds the way humans do, instead of this deep, consuming, instinct-level connection that makes me want to rip her boyfriend into tiny shreds, then drag her off to a cave where I can keep her and my cub safe forever.

I'm ragged from so little sleep because I spend most of my off-hours watching over Dee. Her belly gets visibly bigger, and it just makes me hunger for her even more. That's my young growing in there, and I want nothing more than to be there and help her through it.

Sometimes I come very close to revealing myself, but at this point, that would absolutely ruin any chances I might have with her. It's much too late to tell her that I'm "Bill," and I've been lying to her this whole time.

That I'm the one who fucked her full of cub until she screamed, and now I want them both in my life, forever.

It's late one night, my night off from work, when I see shadows shift inside Dee's apartment. She stands up, rouses Boomer, and leads him away from the sliding glass to the front door. Then she exits the building and comes down the stairs with him clipped to a leash, wearing her pajamas.

She's going on a walk in the middle of the night?

I'm crouched in the bushes that take up most of the yard across the street from her house. Often I'm on the roof, but tonight I was unusually tired and didn't want to make the climb. I might fall and wake the occupants, and then it would be a whole thing.

"I do what I want, *Robbie*," I barely hear her mutter. I wonder if it's fizzling out between them. Maybe then I could make a move as Russ.

Luckily, instead of heading toward me, Dee takes an immediate left and goes down the street. Good. Boomer, much to my delight and my misfortune, has very keen senses. He can see when I move, even from across the street in the darkness. As a wolfman, I have good night vision, but his is impeccable.

I keep a good two blocks behind them as Dee and Boomer navigate toward the park. I'm concerned that she thinks it's a good idea to go for a stroll in such an open and secluded area in the dead of night, where anyone could lay their hands on her.

I wonder if she does this when I'm not around. That sends a shiver up my spine.

I wait until Dee's descended into the darkness of the trees before I cross the last street. It will be harder to see her in here without alerting her to my presence—or Boomer. But I need to stay close and keep her within sight.

Eventually she stops, and sits down at a bench near the open, grassy area. She sighs and leans her head back, and Boomer drops his chin on her knee.

I'm glad she has him when I'm not here.

It doesn't seem like she's going to move anytime soon, so I go a little closer, just to get a good look at her in the moonlight.

Dee is beautiful. She's beautiful, and funny, and feels so

deeply. I think that loving her could truly be wonderful if I got the chance.

I want to get even nearer, but that would be risky, so I come to a stop here and crouch down. But my foot has landed on a twig, and when I apply my weight to it, it snaps in half.

Boomer leaps up to his feet and barks wildly. Dee squeaks as his leash goes taut and he lunges in my direction.

"Boomer!" she cries out. "What is it?"

Boomer tugs harder on the leash, and fear fills Dee's eyes.

"What is it, buddy?" she says, voice trembling. "Who's out there?"

Shit. She's absolutely terrified. I can't let her think some creep is in the park, waiting to jump on her.

Well, I guess there's one creep out here.

"It's me," I say in as calm of a voice as I can as I rise to my feet, still hidden in the shadows. "It's just me, my dear."

"I know your voice," Dee says, furrowing her brow. Then her mouth falls open. "Bill? Is that you?"

I take a step forward, and then another, until finally I'm out from under the shadow of the trees. The moonlight skates across my snout, illuminating my face. Boomer sniffs the air, and his barking stops.

Confusion twists Dee's small features. "Wait, Russ?"

Boomer runs up to me, this time with his tail wagging. He remembers me. I kneel down in front of him to pet his head, hoping to keep myself as unimposing of a figure as possible.

She called me *Bill*.

"Wh-what are you... what are you doing here?" Dee tugs on Boomer's leash, urging him to come back to her. "It's the middle of the night!"

I swallow hard. Fuck. This is the worst possible way this could have gone.

"I'm sorry," I say, extending one hand toward her. She flinches back, her blue eyes gigantic. "I'm so sorry for scaring you, Dee."

She blinks at me when I speak. "Your voice. I thought it was familiar."

All I can do is nod. "I'm Bill," I say, before she can beat me to it.

She pulls Boomer closer to her. "And you've been Bill all along," she whispers. "Russ, you knew. The whole time."

My dirty laundry is out there now, on full display.

"Have you been... following me?" Her words are horrified.

"I had no choice," I say, hoping, begging that she'll understand. "When we met at DreamTogether, Dee, something happened. We connected. I know you felt it, too."

She shudders, and her grip on the leash tightens.

"I felt something," she admits, turning her head away so she doesn't have to look me in the eyes.

That buoys me. That gives me hope.

"I'm sorry that I had to follow you," I say. "But I have to protect you. I have to make sure you and the cub are safe." She may not understand, but I had no choice. Everything in my world is driving me toward her. She and our cub are the pinnacle of my existence.

"And that's why you've been tailing me?" Dee asks, voice pitching high as she turns back to glare at me. "You're following me around in a park at night to *protect* me?" Then, it's as if she realizes something, the way her mouth falls open. "That's why you were there, isn't it? When you saved Boomer?"

Again, I nod, because there's no point in trying to lie anymore.

"Bill," she murmurs, as I rise back to my feet. Dee stares up at me as I block out the moon from touching her face. "I never thought I'd see you again, and you... you've been here the whole time."

And then, quite suddenly, tears burst from her eyes. She raises a fist and charges at me, and I stumble back in surprise as she slams it into my chest.

"You fucking psycho!" she wails. "You could have just said, 'Hey, Dee, remember me? Bill?' and I would have jumped into your lap!" I catch her arm in my big paw, and she struggles to keep hitting me with it. She's crying harder now, and I'm worried someone's going to think I'm assaulting her and send the cops. "Instead, though," Dee growls, "you had to go and fucking *stalk me!*"

I'm a fool. A complete idiot. I should never have lied to her when she mentioned DreamTogether. I'd been too afraid of that stupid boyfriend of hers, of how she might turn me away, as if he holds any candle to the mating bond I share with Dee.

"I'm sorry," I whisper. "I wish I'd told you the truth. But I didn't want to get in the way of your life." With my hand wrapped around hers, I tug her closer to me, and she stumbles forward. She's stopped trying to hit me, at least, but she's still holding firm against me.

"I would have dropped everything for you," she says with a hiccup. "This could have all been different. Do you know how much I've thought about you? How much I've wished you were here?"

I reach out to stroke her cheek and she whimpers, the tears still flowing fast. This must be a shock with how overwhelming her emotions already are.

"I'm here now," I say, flicking some of her tears away with my thumb claw. Dee's huge eyes are spiderwebbed with red as she fervently shakes her head. "I've always been here, and I always will be."

But when I say this, her eyes get even bigger. "Every time Boomer barked, that was because of you?" she asks, shaking her head in disbelief, her lips twisting. "You've been following me... for *months*?"

I nod slowly, not objecting to her raining down judgment on me. I will bear any punishment if it means we can come out on the other side.

"He's a good dog," is all I can say to defend myself. "You chose well. I'm glad you have him when I couldn't be there."

But Dee's tears only come faster now. "You should have been there!" she cries. "You could have been there the whole time!"

"It's not too late." I curl my hand around her head and gently pull her toward me. At first she resists, but as I simply let her cry, she falls into me, burying her face in my fur and getting it all wet. Despite her objections, though, her hands are already roaming across my body, sliding up my back and tangling in the fur of my mane. Her scent changes, shifting from sour anxiety to a sweet, rampant desire.

I'm elated that I can elicit the same need in her that she does in me. What's wafting up to my nose is unlike anything in the world, like one cloud in a perfect blue sky. Her smell is blooming, and my body is already answering its siren call. My fingers slide down her back, over the curve of her incredible ass, and her body jolts. I breathe her in, filling my nose with her, licking my lips while I think of everything I've wanted to do to her for months.

"I've longed for nothing but you," I murmur in her ear as I draw a hand around her waist, then slide it over her swollen belly. Instinctually, her hips rise into mine, and I cradle where my cub is growing inside her. "My every waking thought has been consumed by you."

"Me... me too," she whimpers, pushing my hand down from her belly button toward her flannel pajama pants. "I can't stop thinking about you, no matter how hard I try." She's shivering underneath me, her body responding to mine as I drag one finger over her mound, toward that blistering warm place at the crux of her thighs. That's where I'm meant to be.

"Stop trying," I murmur to her, "and let me in."

In response, Dee presses into me, her pelvis grinding against my hand. Nearby, Boomer lets out a whine. I dip my finger lower, so I'm brushing over the layers of clothing between me and her perfect cunt. Her own hands wind down my hips, on top of my jeans, and she whimpers when I drag the pad of my finger down her seam where it's hidden underneath her clothes. Instantly, the fabric turns warm, and I can already feel her wetness through it.

"Damn it," she says, wriggling her hips to gain even more friction against my hand. "Stop teasing me and... and..."

"And what?" I ask, and it comes out a throaty growl. "Should I tear these off, right now?" I tighten my paws, digging my claws into her clothing, and her thighs squeeze around my hand. Under my finger, her sweet pussy pulses faster, hotter.

"Yes!" She's grinding herself against me, her body telling me exactly what it wants. "Please!"

The wetness is seeping through her pants now, and Dee's breaths speed up. My cock has already emerged from my sheath inside my jeans, and I'm more than ready to be welcomed into her wet warmth again. Oh, fuck, how I've needed her more than anything else.

"Then I'm going to remind you what it feels like to take wolfman cock." I puncture her clothes with one claw and then rip, tearing her pants and underwear apart right down the middle. She squeaks, but before she can move, I'm dragging my knuckle all over her clit. A tremor travels through Dee's small form as I dance across her sensitive, tiny bead, again and again.

"Remind me," she breathes.

With my other hand, I unzip my own jeans, shoving them down my hips and tail. I'm not going to wait a moment longer. Not that I need to—I find my woman is slick for me already when I taste her soft folds with my knuckle, each petal decorated with fine hair. My eyes roll back in my head at just this sample, and I find the urge to lock my teeth in her shoulder almost overwhelming.

But I need to be careful with her and not get carried away.

With my leaking cock exposed, I press my bare groin to her lower back. She lifts her hips until she's standing on her toes, fitting my length between her thighs. "I can't do it anymore," she says, her voice helpless. "I need you, right now."

It sends a burst of flame racing through my body, hearing how desperate she is for me. I bend my knees so my cock can slide between her thighs and obediently, Dee spreads her legs. I glide across her wet sex, and it's quickly driving me to madness.

"Wait." She's panting. "I... I want to look at you this time."

This woman is going to fucking kill me. I snatch her by the hips and turn her toward me, and she tilts her head up to gaze into my face. Her blue eyes are big, and her cheeks are a bright, flushed red, her pink-brown lips parted. I don't realize I've been holding her up off the ground until she lifts her legs and winds them around my hips. I hook both my hands under her ass, and there's so much hot blood coursing through me that taking on her entire body's weight feels like nothing.

Now my cock is trapped between us, the pink length of it sprawled across her swelled belly. Just the sight of this evidence of my cub inside her, poking out from under her shirt, makes my balls throb.

Her tongue darts out, licking her lips as she follows my line of sight down to where we're almost connected. Her face goes slack.

"That's what it looks like," she whispers, and my lips curl in a self-satisfied smirk. Drool drips from my fangs and lands on her soft, rounded stomach.

"Both of you are mine," I growl. Dee doesn't confirm or deny it, but she doesn't need to. Even if she doesn't accept it, it's the truth—no one will ever get between me and my mate ever again.

I can't wait a second longer. I heft her up easily, so her ankles are hooked over my hips, and the sloped head of my cock is pointing of its own accord at the soaked place between her legs. She shines in the moonlight, red and swollen for me. It takes all of my self-restraint not to simply impale her on my dick. Instead, I push through her outer folds and into the warm cavern waiting there, trying to hold back.

Dee moans immediately and clenches tight, even though I'm barely inside her. I shut my eyes hard, hoping I can move slow enough not to hurt her while all my instincts demand I drown myself in that divine pussy *right now*. I push deeper, asking for even more, and her pliant little body gives to me.

"Oh, fuck," she mutters, winding her arms around my neck. I peer down my snout at her, and the unguarded need on her face ignites something in me. I squeeze her ass tighter, my claws sinking into her flesh as my cock slips farther into her. She cries out, but it's pleasure, not pain, pouring from her soft mouth.

I need her to stay quiet, though, so I lean my head down and my long tongue darts out, tracing the junction of her lips. Dee's eyes fly wide as I find an opening and invade her mouth the same way my cock is invading her cunt. Her muffled moan drives me even deeper inside her until my knot is teasing at her taut edges. I continue fucking her with my tongue as I pull my slick cock out, nearly leaving her completely. She whines against me, as if even this small distance between us is not acceptable. And it isn't, not now that I have her in my arms.

I explore even deeper into her mouth as I drive in once more, returning home to her, staking my claim on her. She is mine, and I'll make sure she knows it for as long as she lives.

sixteen

DEE

IT IS the most debauched thing possible to be enjoying myself as Bill's tongue reaches my throat, his fanged jaws wide open above my face. He could clamp down on my head at any time, but I know he never would. I am literally inside the lion's jaws, making out with him while he fucks me into a whimpering, sweating, mindless puddle. My legs are wrapped like iron around his waist, his huge, clawed hands holding me up in the air as he guides himself in and out of me, that immense, fat cock pushing every limit I have. I'm helpless in his arms as he brings me down onto him again and again, squeezing my ass in his claws so tight I wonder if I'll have marks later.

I couldn't care any less.

My Bill. *No, it's Russ.* Fuck, it doesn't matter. He smells like home, and having him inside me again is simply arriving back where I belong. My brain is light and airy, filled with his scent, with the heady delirium of having him inside me again.

I whimper and cry and wrap my arms even tighter around his neck, burying my fingers in his scruff with each mad thrust. That amazing cock of his is winding me up, spinning my pleasure around me into a whirlwind. I sob into his huge mouth as he glides on a river of both our fluids, that bulbous knot of his hinting again and again at what it would like to do.

His tongue snakes back out of my mouth, and there's drool covering my face.

"I'm going to fuck my knot into you," he says in that low, rumbling voice. "I'm going to stretch you wide, until your pussy can't be filled by anyone else but me."

My brain is foggy, so foggy with my bliss, that all I can do is moan, "Yes!"

He pumps his hips faster, harder, that bulge starting to squeeze into me with each deep stroke. As he commanded, I'm opening for him, allowing through a little more each time. The more I accommodate him, the greater the volley of pleasure that echoes through me, from my throat to my toes. Bill—no, *Russ*—shoves into me harder, and I buckle forward. He lowers his nose to touch it to mine, and I open my eyes to gaze up at him.

His irises are bright amber, his black pupils blown out and huge. The skin is bunched up on his snout in a vicious snarl, his teeth bared with each plunge inside me. More of his knot is working its way in, and I'm so full that I might simply pop like a balloon.

"Take it," he rumbles. "Take my knot. Take all of me."

"I will," I sob, and then the rest of his thick, swollen cock finally slips through. But that's not what sends me over the edge, tumbling into oblivion—it's when he yanks it free, then shoves it into me a second, a third, a fourth time, that my body can't take any more, and my orgasm shatters me.

I bury my face into the fur of his throat and scream as it shakes me like an earthquake. My wolfman groans as he slides in one final time, and then I'm clamped around him so tight, he can't pull out again. He makes a strangled sound, almost like a kicked dog, and then he swells. Suddenly, teeth sink into the flesh of my shoulder, and the exquisite pain of the bite morphs into a mad, impossible pleasure, ratcheting up my climax into another mountain.

Then he explodes. His hot come fills me up in a rush so powerful I feel it slosh inside me, asking me to make even more room. Whimpering, he thrusts again, burying himself even deeper. As his own peak consumes him, his pumps grow shallower, and there's a wet *squelch* as his excess spills out around his knot. Panting, he finally falls limp. Then he stumbles backwards, still buried in me, and comes to rest against a tree trunk.

I gasp for air, clinging to him like my life depends on it. He holds me around my ass, his knot stuck like a stopper, his jaws sunk into the flesh of my shoulder. Ever so slowly he releases me, and then the acute, painful sting of it finally hits.

"Ow, fuck," I say, reaching up to cover the wound.

"I'm so sorry." Russ stands up straighter and peers down at the damage he's done. "I didn't mean to do that. I wasn't going to do that." His cock twitches inside me.

"What is it? What did you do?"

"It's my mark," he says quietly. "Because you're my mate, and I had to—"

"I'm your *what?*"

Oh, fuck. Fuck, fuck, fuck.

Some monsters, like wolfmen and yetis and orcs, have life mates. I've heard people say it's spiritual, supernatural,

LYONNE RILEY

fated by a higher power. Others believe it's simply hormones and instincts and genetic compatibility.

But Russ has decided I'm his mate...

"I knew it after the first time," he says, then pauses to lick the wound. It stings, but also strangely, feels good. "You're mine, Dee. You and the cub both."

He's speaking too fast, so fast I can't keep up.

"Now that you know the truth," he continues, his voice frantic, "you should move into my house, and—"

What the fuck is he saying? "Stop," I snap, tensing up all over. With his knot still trapped inside my tight pussy, he groans. "I'm not yours, Bill. Russ. Whoever you are. And I'm not *moving* anywhere." I try to separate myself from him, because now, suddenly, I realize how desperately we need to have an actual conversation.

I can't believe I just *flung* myself at him that way. I'm such a moron. I guess just another animal fueled by instinct and base needs.

Russ whimpers as I try to pull his knot free of me. "Dee," he says in a worried voice. "You can't move yet." He remains holding me up with one arm, and wraps the other around my back to keep me close to him. "I just want to make sure you're safe. And the two of you will be safest if you're with me."

I push away again, and this time, his knot has gone down enough that he slips free of me. I wriggle out of his arms and drop to the ground, and Russ stares down at me, his brow furrowed in concern.

"I'm not going anywhere," I say, planting both my feet firmly. "I have my own apartment. I have a..."

I have a boyfriend.

Oh, extra fucks. I just had sex with a wolfman who thinks I'm his life mate, while Robbie's probably at home, fast asleep in his bed. It just... completely exited my brain. Like there was nothing else in the world that mattered except being with Bill again.

Has he brainwashed me?

"Dee, please." Russ kneels down at my feet, his soaking-wet cock hanging limp between his legs. He's still level with my chest even like this, and he reaches out one hand to touch me. I jerk back in surprise. "Let me be there for you. Let me watch over you and our cub. You can have anything you need, and then we'll raise it together, and—"

He's fucking delusional.

"You're crazy," I say, blinking back tears. I take a step back. "Raise it together? What are you talking about?" He has a whole world up there in his head that's separate from mine. He wants a relationship, a family. That's why he came to DreamTogether in the first place.

Now that the high of sex and lust has faded, I comb back over everything Russ said and did after the dog attack. Now, I understand why he gave me his number, why he checked in on me over text message in a way that felt so sweet and genuine.

"So that's it," I say quietly, as horror dawns on me. "You didn't want to be my friend. You were... you were trying to ingratiate yourself in my life." My voice is strained and broken. "You were going to try to break up Robbie and I, weren't you?"

When Russ's mouth falls open, I know that I'm right. Even worse, he was living a double life—one as Russ, my friend, and one as Bill, my stalker. Little pieces in my memory click into place, of a car that looked vaguely like Russ's behind me in traffic, of someone walking a few blocks behind me as I went on a walk. Boomer going wild in the middle of the night.

How did he even find me? DreamTogether is supposed to be completely anonymous. He had nothing to go on, and managed to track me down.

Then... he bit me. While he was inside me, he fucking *bit me* to make me his mate, when I never agreed to anything like that.

It's honestly terrifying. And maybe it's even worse that I went along with this, that I *wanted* this.

Shivering, I pull Boomer closer to me. My pants are a mess, and Russ's come is slipping down my thighs in a river. I'm disgusted with myself.

"I just want you to be safe," Russ says in a pleading tone. "That human guy can't do that. That's not his cub, it's mine. I can watch over you. I can be—"

"Shut up!" It bursts out of me, much louder than I intended, but I'm filling with rage. "You are a fucking creep. You could have told me the truth so long ago, but you didn't. No, instead you made me feel paranoid. You lied about so many things, made me believe you were someone else."

And I just fucking had sex with him. Carnal, primal, mind-blowing sex.

"I'm so sorr—" Russ opens his mouth to say, but I smack him right in the snout. His head swings to one side and I back away, Boomer's leash clutched tight in my hand. His mouth falls open as he turns back to face me, his eyes wide and betrayed.

I can't believe I just did that. But I'm not just enraged by what he's done—I'm furious at myself, too, for falling for it. Why did he have to lie to me? Now I can't trust him.

"Come on, boy," I tell Boomer, then turn around and jog away, fresh tears stinging behind my eyes.

"Wait!" Russ's claws click on the sidewalk as he starts after me. "Dee!"

I glance back over my shoulder at the wolfman standing in the middle of the path, his jeans at his feet. The devastation is clear on his face as I leave him behind.

I don't care how I feel about Russ, I tell myself. I don't care how much that look makes me hurt, how obvious it is that I mean the world to him. I don't care how fierce and right it felt to be with him. None of that matters.

He's... he's dangerous. All red flags. And I need to get away from him as fast as I can, for my sake and this baby's.

RUSS

Watching Dee run away, her pants ripped from front to back and hanging in shreds, will be forever imprinted on my memory. The agony I feel, knowing I can't chase her or I'll only reinforce what she already believes.

What she already *knows*. Because it's the truth, really.

I am a fucking creep.

When she's gone, I fall to the ground on my knees. Fuck. I really ruined it. I ruined everything.

I can't help it when my head tilts back, my nose points up at the moon, and a mournful howl pours from my mouth. It's all I can do, calling out to the world just how unfair it is that I'd be bound to her, and she wouldn't want me in return.

Well, she might have, if I hadn't royally screwed up every part of it I could.

My mate. My cub.

My whole world.

seventeen

DEE

ANOTHER POWERFUL, even sadder howl fills the night air as I jog the last block to my duplex. It strains at the edges of my heart, making it feel tight and squeezed. A shiver runs down my spine, and for a moment, I feel compelled to turn around and run back to him.

I didn't want to leave, but it was the right thing to do. Tomorrow, I'll probably need to get law enforcement involved.

I don't want that, either. But is Russ even... sane? I rub the spot where he bit me, and my hand comes away red with blood. *My* blood.

If I were smart, I'd get a restraining order. But my heart seizes at the thought that I might not see Russ again if I went through with it.

Our cub, he kept saying. I hate that it sounded good. How many times have I thought about Bill and wished that I could find him again, that he would see the way my belly has grown with his child and love it the way Robbie never will?

He wants so badly to watch over us and keep us safe that he followed me for months. He wants me, all of me, in his life. In a way, it's profoundly hot—but it's also very, very dangerous. The alarm bells are going off in my head, and I should listen to them.

I can't be his mate, as much as he believes I am.

When I finally get back to the house, I usher Boomer inside then jump into the shower. There, the soreness sets in from when Russ stretched me wide, because I haven't used the dilator in weeks. I scrub myself clean, especially the sticky mess between my thighs, then get out and throw my torn clothes in the garbage. When I'm showered and dressed in fresh pajamas, I climb into bed, Boomer taking his usual place at my feet.

But I don't sleep, not for hours still. All my nerve endings are on high alert, and I can still feel echoes of how Russ felt, deep inside me.

He could still be outside my window, right now, watching me. Keeping an eye on me and our baby.

Strangely, that last thought is what lulls me to sleep.

The next day I don't wake until nearly noon, and I'm groggy when I finally get up. It's only Boomer's whines that pull me out of bed because he needs to go outside.

Wearing my bathrobe, I go down the steps with him to the greenway and he relieves himself. I peer around to see if Russ is there, but he must have done a good job of hiding if I didn't see him before now.

"Let me get cleaned up and we'll go out," I tell Boomer as we head back to the apartment.

I need to make some calls, too, but not right away. I should take time to think about what happened last night, and what I'm going to do about it.

Unfortunately, the first thing to cross my mind when I head out with Boomer on a leash is that I have to tell Robbie. That's going to be an ugly conversation that I don't want to have. Should I admit to him that I fucked someone else before I dump him? Or is that just twisting a knife that doesn't need to be twisted?

Man. I'm an asshole.

I text Robbie asking to see him, trying not to make it sound ominous. It's not that I want to take him by surprise, but I also don't want him dreading what I'll have to say.

We don't usually go out to eat, but I suggest a Greek restaurant.

> I didn't know you liked Greek food.

The text message makes me laugh because there's so, so much that Robbie doesn't know about me.

Then I call up Liesel. I need to decide if I'm in danger, if I have to start thinking about reporting Russ to Dream-Together.

Would they keep his baby from him? I can't do that.

Liesel's at work, but she answers on the first ring anyway.

"I have to talk to you," I say before she can even get out a greeting.

"What about?" Liesel asks, without skipping a beat. "Do you need me to come over?"

"Now? I mean, that would be great, but aren't you at work?"

I can almost hear her shrug on the other end. "They won't miss me for an hour."

So I agree, and heat some hot water in the kettle for herbal tea, which is all I can really drink. Then I pour it over ice, because it's fucking hot out, and wait at the table until Liesel knocks at the door.

For a second I'm afraid to answer it, in case it's Russ on the other side. Would he come back after last night, even though I made myself clear that I don't want to see him again?

But when I peer through the peephole, I find Liesel standing on the other side. I open the door with a sigh of relief—but maybe also disappointment.

"What's going on?" Liesel asks, helping herself to one of the two glasses of iced tea on the table. She surveys me up and down. "You look... tired."

I suppose that's one way to describe it. It's more like a bone-deep exhaustion. Everything changed in one night and now I'm adrift, even more than before.

"Remember Russ?" I ask, and Liesel blinks at me.

"Russ?"

"The wolfman who saved Boomer."

She nods and sips her tea. "Right."

I launch into the whole sordid story of how he gave me the cream, how he was becoming my friend. How I found out last night he'd been following me—and that he's also Bill.

As usual, Liesel's face doesn't give away much. "So that's who that wolfman at my office was," she says, with a *hmm*.

My heart skips. "What wolfman at your office?"

"When I was leaving work one day, this wolfman came up to me asking about someone with a ridiculous fake name. I bet that was him trying to pick up your scent."

My very skin shivers. He even used Liesel to get to me?

"What did you do when you found out?" my friend asks,

but the tone of her voice makes it sound like she already knows the answer. Still, her eyebrows rise a little higher when I confess that we fucked in the park.

"I feel like I lost my mind out there," I say, giving Boomer a guilty look because he had to witness it all. "I just... I couldn't help it."

"So you went feral?" Liesel asks.

"I mean, that's one word you could use," I say uncertainly. Though *feral* is a pretty accurate description of what Russ did to me with his cock.

"No, as in, the medical term."

"What?"

She sighs. "When mate-bond species find their mates, they go 'feral.' It's an out-of-control state. Basically, all you want to do is have sex."

That sounds like last night, for sure. I was absolutely wild for him, even when I knew it was a bad idea.

"But that can't happen to humans, right?" I ask, frowning.

"Of course it can happen to us. We're animals, too."

"Humans don't form mate-bonds, though." That's the problem—or one of them. What Russ feels for me, that instinct-level attachment, I won't ever feel it the way he does.

Liesel quirks an eyebrow. "How do you know that?" she asks. "His pheromones are designed to bond the two of you. His body is probably sending yours all sorts of messages, if you're really his mate."

I hate all this science-y mumbo jumbo.

"So what?" I ask. "So we had sex. So I was out of my mind. That doesn't mean I can't see the whole picture for what it really is, which is super fucked up. Russ has been stalking me!" I throw back a bunch of iced tea like it's a strong cocktail. "He said all this crap about how he wants to *protect us*, and demanded I move in, and—"

"That's coming on a little strong," Liesel remarks.

"No shit."

She leans back in her chair. "You know, I think I watched something about this on an episode of *Wild World.*" She pulls out her phone and types something in. "A-ha." She scrolls a page on the phone, reading. "Just what I thought."

She hands the phone over to me, and I glance over the headline of the page: AGGRESSION IN MATED WOLF-MEN. It's a scientific article, with a short brief right below it.

I snatch the phone away from her and start reading.

"This study followed two dozen wolfmen throughout the stages of mating. Not all wolfpeople meet a mate in their lifetime, but when they do, mating triggers a powerful rush of chemicals and hormones designed to help the wolfman protect his mate and offspring from rivals, predators, and other dangers. In modern civilization, this can manifest in acts of aggression, fierce rutting, territorial fighting, and in the event of conception, even more dangerous behaviors. Wolfmen were ten times as likely during the onset of mating to display aggression until the bond was secured. In the event of pregnancy, they all insisted on keeping their mates close for the duration. Some couples in the study sought counseling, while others weathered the storm."

I hand the phone back to her, silent. Damn. So Russ's crazy isn't limited to just him.

Still, though, that doesn't excuse what he did. Lying to me? Following me? *Watching* me?

"Are you saying I should give him a pass?" I ask Liesel. "Just because he thinks I'm his mate?"

"He doesn't *think* you're his mate," she says. "He knows you are. You wouldn't have gone feral last night unless your body and hormones were feeling it, too."

I shudder all over. "It's not a choice?" I ask. "I'm human. It should be a choice for me."

Liesel tilts her head. "Well, you don't have to accept it. It's not driving you to do stupid things like follow a pregnant woman around at night and try to out-nice guy her boyfriend. You just don't have to see him again, and it won't go any further. Not for you, anyway. You'll be able to move on with your life."

I ask a question, even though I'm dreading the answer. "But for him?"

"Well, he's mated now," Liesel says with a shrug. "Even if the bond is never secured."

"And... that's it?" I wonder what that means, that it will never *secure*.

She goes back to her phone and does some more research. "This says that in the event the mate bond never secures—in the event of death or rejection—the wolfman will typically live his life out alone. Some found temporary partners, but it never lasted. And they often returned to the homes of their mates, sometimes in their sleep."

"That's fucked up," I whisper, mostly to myself, and I shudder all over. "Really? That's... that's it for Russ? *Me?*" That's not fair to him—not at all.

And it's not fair to me, either. It means that unless I want Russ to be alone forever, then I'm all he has.

And our cub, I can almost hear him say. I shudder. Why does that sound so *good*? While Robbie tries to pretend my belly doesn't exist, Russ worshipped it.

Liesel pockets her phone. "What are you going to do?"

"What do you mean?" I ask, frowning. "He's crazy. He was hiding in the fucking trees when I was walking alone in a park at night."

"Which was kind of stupid of you," says Liesel.

"So what?" I want to stomp my feet. "I should be allowed to do it without being afraid someone's following me."

"But you know Russ would never hurt you."

I'm surprised that she's taking his side. But I know she's right, too. Russ would never put me in harm's way, not the kind, gentle friend who brought me cream from the hospital, who told me not to be angry at myself for things I can't control, who was there for me when no one else could be in the way I needed. He delivers babies, for fuck's sake.

But then I remember. "He bit me, Liesel." I pull down the collar of my shirt to show her the angry red scabs on my shoulder. "He said he was *marking* me."

"That was one of the symptoms on the list, so I'm not surprised," she says. "He didn't ask you first?"

I frown. "No! We were in the middle of, well, you know."

She nods sagely. "Heat of the moment."

I squint at Liesel. "You think I should forgive him," I say, as a statement and not a question.

Her neutral expression finally gives way to something that looks almost like pity. "I think you should do what you want to do," she says, more fervently. "Not what you *have* to do."

"What I *have* to do," I say, "is break up with Robbie tonight. And then maybe I can decide what to do about Russ."

Liesel nods. "I believe that is a smart course of action." She gets to her feet, and offers me the slightest smile. "You'll be okay, Dee. You know how to take care of yourself. But think hard about what will actually make you happy."

When Liesel's finally gone, I sit down at the table and my hand drops to my belly. *Little guy, it's a tricky world out here,* I think. What will become of this baby once it's all over?

It belongs to Russ, I suppose. Not me.

Let me watch over you and our cub. We'll raise it together.

That's what he wants. He wants a wife and a child, a mate and a cub, like every wolfman before him. But this was supposed to be simple. I was supposed to have the baby and then be done, wipe my hands of it and walk away free. I never agreed to start a family with him. That wasn't what I wanted out of this, not at all.

Then why does it sound so *good*?

After I've watered the plants—which have multiplied in great numbers, and I've had to separate out a few into new pots—my phone buzzes. It's Robbie, letting me know he's on the way to the restaurant.

Fuck. None of that other stuff matters until I resolve this.

eighteen

RUSS

I DON'T GO BACK to Dee's house the next day. It takes all of my willpower not to drive my familiar route to her neighborhood, to make sure that she and the cub are all right after last night. I wasn't gentle with her, when maybe I should have been.

But she won't want to see me. And as soon as Boomer barks, she'll know I'm there, violating her space.

Damn it. How did I fuck this up so badly?

Instead of going to Dee's house, I get in my car and head north. I drive an hour, then two, until I reach the Sandy Hill Wilderness Area. It's all wild terrain out here, not managed by any of the parks departments.

And it's one of the only legal places I can go hunting. I have far too much pent-up hurt inside me, an ocean of self-pity, and this is the only way I can get it out without tracking down my woman and fucking her again wherever I find her.

I pull over to the side of the road when I can't take it any longer. After having Dee last night, she's the only thing in my thoughts. I can feel her soft body in my arms, her sweet pussy clenching around me, her hands woven through my fur.

I let out an unbridled roar of fury when I remember how she told me in no uncertain terms that I was not welcome in her life any longer, that our connection doesn't mean to her what it does to me.

Will I spend the rest of my years longing for her, wishing for her, and I won't get to have her? Raising our cub without her...

I hastily take off my shirt and my jeans, my hands trembling, then fold them up and leave them in my car with the key on top. If someone wants to steal it, fine. I don't care anymore.

With a final deep breath, I fall down to four legs and lope away into the woods.

The scent of pine fills up my nose as I dive into the trees. The brush is thick here, overgrown, and the fallen needles crinkle under my feet. I run and run, sniffing the air, checking out trees where animals might have been. I pick up the scent of some rabbits, but that's not what I'm after.

I need something big, something dangerous, something that will make me battle for my victory. If I can't drown myself in Dee, I'll drown myself in blood.

Then, I stumble upon it: the musk of a deer, a whole herd of them. My mouth waters, and the hair on my back bristles as I search for the direction it's coming from. I lope onward, catching the scent again on a tree trunk, where some bark has been torn away.

It doesn't take me long to trace their scent back to them. In a small clearing stand three does and one stag, followed by two fawns, as they munch on grasses. I crouch and lick my lips, my claws extending even further.

If I can't have my woman, if I can't have my growing cub near me, then I will destroy.

I leap out of the trees in a single burst, landing on the stag's back. I want a fight. I want prey that will make me work for it.

The other deer scatter, but as the stag tries to get away, I bury my claws in its back. We're evenly matched for size, but he has big antlers and sharp hooves, which he uses as he tries to buck me off and kick me. I get a hoof to the thigh and I let out a howl of pain, but don't let go.

Lifting my head high, I open my jaws wide, then bury my teeth in the stag's throat. With a scream that sounds almost human, the animal fights harder, and I use all the force in my body to clamp down tight. But I'm making a rookie mistake by trying to bite from the back of the neck and not the vulnerable underside. There's too much dense muscle here.

Releasing my hold on the stag, it manages to throw me. But I still have one claw lodged in it, and I manage to bring it down to the ground with me. While it struggles to get back to its feet, I'm on it in a millisecond, diving for the exposed throat.

This time, I squeeze down hard, and the stag wails. As my teeth sink in deep, blood fills my mouth. I groan at the taste, at the warmth of it trickling down my tongue. I hold on like that until the stag stops moving underneath me.

When I draw back, a trail of blood follows me, and I lick it off my teeth. Then I bury my face in the hot flesh, blood still pumping through the stag's veins. As I tear and rip, separating flesh from bone, I must be covered in the stuff.

I don't know how long I lose myself in my prey like that, in a mindless, instinctual haze. By the time I feel so full I could be sick, the sun has started to set. I leave the carcass there and lazily walk through the woods, back to my car.

I don't even bother putting my clothes back on. I'm probably tracking blood all over my leather seats, but I don't give a shit.

I put the car in reverse and back into the road, then turn the wheel and roar off the way I came.

DEE

Robbie's car is already parked out front when I get to the Greek restaurant. I'm dreading this conversation, and I don't even know what I'm going to tell him yet.

Sorry, man, but my baby daddy's walked back into my life and said I'm his forever mate. Oh, did I mention he's a wolfman, and then we fucked in the park in the middle of the night?

When I walk in, Robbie's sitting in the far back of the restaurant at a little corner table. He hasn't ordered a drink, which is unusual for him. He waves when I walk up, and gets out of his chair to kiss me.

Fuck. What do I do? If I don't kiss him back, he'll know I'm about to dump him.

I turn it into as light of a peck as I can before slipping into my seat. Robbie replaces his napkin on his lap.

"No glass of wine?" I ask. "Or a beer?"

Robbie smiles. "You can't, so I realized I haven't been very considerate of you. I decided I'm going to quit drinking, too, until you have the baby."

Oh, jeez. It's thoughtful and sweet, and also a gesture he could have made months ago.

"Wow. Thanks. You don't have to do that, though. It doesn't bother me."

He shakes his head. "Solidarity. You've also been getting such a nice butt lately from walking Boomer all the time, I think I'm going to take up jogging."

I sure hope he keeps all these New Years resolutions after I've told him it's over.

"Robbie." I have to do it now, before we're an appetizer and two meals deep. I'll foot the bill if I have to from guilt, but I would rather not continue this conversation longer than we have to. "That's all very sweet of you, but it's not necessary. I mean, you should definitely jog if you want to."

He smiles, and it pierces my gut.

"I just feel like we haven't been seeing each other as much lately, and I wondered if it's because you feel like you're alone in so many things."

Damn it. He's not about to finally have the emotional depth I've been hoping he would have all along, is he?

"Robbie..." I begin again.

"No, no. I know you've been going through a lot with the aches and pains and the insomnia," he says. "And I feel like I could be a much more supportive boyfriend."

Fuck.

"Robbie!" I interrupt him more firmly this time. The waiter stops next to our table, and Robbie's about to order when I wave him away. "Two more minutes," I say. "I haven't even gotten to look at the menu yet." When the waiter's gone, Robbie has a wide-eyed look on his face. "I'm sorry. Before you continue, I need to talk to you about something."

His face slackens. "Shit."

Neither of us has to say it for him to know that I'm about to break up with him. It must be obvious on my face.

"I'm sorry," I say. "But something came up, and—"

"What kind of 'something'?" he asks, and I can already hear his voice cracking. I can't look into his huge, green-brown eyes right now.

"I haven't told you everything." I weave my hands together in front of me and stare down at them instead. "I'm not just carrying a regular human baby. I'm carrying, um... a wolfman's baby."

I don't have to look up to imagine his expression.

"And, um," I barrel onwards, figuring I might as well just rip off the band-aid, "I slept with him. The father. Last night."

Finally, I chance a look up, and Robbie is... not shocked. If anything, he's hurt.

And then, angry.

"You lied to me?" he asks, his cheeks already turning pink. "About the baby?"

"I'm sorry." I squeeze my hands into fists, finding it hard to keep looking at him. "I didn't want you to—"

"To judge you? But you didn't give me the chance, did you? And then you..." He trails off, his face reddening even more as his lips twist. "Then you *fucked him*?"

He says this loud enough that I duck my head and wave at him. "Keep it down," I hiss.

"No." He takes his napkin off his lap and drops it on the table, and his eyes are narrowed in a death glare. "You brought me here to tell me you've been lying to me for months, and then you cheated on me, too?" He gets up, tossing his menu. Other people around the restaurant look up from their meals as Robbie makes a scene. "Good thing I didn't order a drink," he says, and there's a look of disgust on his face I've never seen before. I didn't even know Robbie had it in him.

With that, he strides past me, out of the restaurant. I'm

shocked to find my eyes aching at the corners where tears threaten to fall.

I knew this would go badly, but I didn't predict just how badly. Robbie's been there for me, and I repaid him in the worst way possible.

Man, I was such a shithead.

I drop my head into my hands and cry. The waiter avoids me and the other patrons stare at me as I let it all out, right there at the table. Eventually, I place an order for a gyro to go, and drag myself home feeling like the scum of the earth.

Robbie will never forgive me, I'm sure of it. I'd hoped we might stay friends, but I don't know where I got that hallucination from. Of course he would want nothing to do with me after I betrayed him.

I didn't expect it would hurt so much to say goodbye, and I wish I'd done all of this differently.

Damn it, Russ. Why did he have to be so damn hot? Why did his body have to decide that I was his? Why did mine have to fuck me over by wanting him in return?

If I had just thought for five seconds, maybe.

This could have all been so much less complicated. I was supposed to have this baby, give it back, and then move on with my life. That was the plan; that was the deal. I sure didn't sign up to be a wolfman's mate and raise that baby with him.

But my stomach twists just thinking about not seeing him again, about handing this child over to him and walking away.

I know that after this, Robbie will be angry. He'll cuss me out at home, and drink too much with his friends. But he'll move on, and find another girlfriend, and probably discover his own happiness someday.

Now, however, I have no idea how I could possibly move on from Russ.

nineteen

RUSS

I STAY AWAY, and I stay away, and it slowly eats at me.

When the urge to find her grows too strong, I go on a long, punishing run, or head to the gym. I haven't been working out much at all since I found Dee, and my body has grown weaker in the meantime. I push myself hard for an hour, then two, until I'm panting so heavily my tongue is dripping saliva everywhere. I put more weight on the dead-lift than I should, only to realize I'm thirty-seven in three days and I shouldn't be testing out my limits.

And still, when I get into the shower, it feels like none of the pain or rage or pure, physical need has gone away. I've taken some of the edge off, but it still lurks there just under-neath the surface like a sea monster. Standing under the hot water I grab my stiff cock in one hand and brace myself against the tile.

It's easy to close my eyes and picture Dee in my arms, her mouth in a perfect circle, her breasts jiggling with every one of my thrusts. Her body was flawless, her belly gently swelled with me, and I groan as my orgasm grows nearly unbearable. Then it bursts, and I gasp as my cock spurts out one long trail of come after another.

Fuck. My balls don't feel any better afterwards, and it barely satisfied the animal inside me.

She needs time, that's all. I just have to hope that once the shock has worn off from finding out Bill and I are the same, she'll forgive me.

I need to have her and our cub in my life, or I might just lose my mind.

But days pass, and nothing.

I resist the most powerful urge to call her, to message her, to do anything that might put us in contact again. I just want to see her, or hear her voice. I want to know that our cub is doing well.

Anything.

I think about sending her flowers, or even a simple note to let her know I'm thinking about her. I may be an idiot, but I know none of that will help. It will only drive her farther away if I try to bridge the gap between us.

I've always been dedicated to my work, but it gets harder and harder to focus. I ask to cash in some of my vacation days because I'm concerned about not giving my patients my full, undivided attention.

"I've noticed for a while now that your mood is off," says the head doctor, a keen vampire with hair graying along her hairline. "Get some rest, Dr. Cohen. I want you all fixed up when you return from your week off."

I do my best to follow her orders. For the first few days of my "vacation," I try to go to bed early and sleep in, but it never fails that as soon as the light peers in my window, I'm wide awake and all of my instincts are telling me to *find her. Protect her.*

Damn it. Is it really just mating hormones driving me toward her?

No. I *know* Dee now, and that's how I also know that I love her.

I try to distract myself by seeing friends, but if I'm honest, I'm kind of a drag.

"Wish I could help more," Caleb says, rubbing the side of his big head. He's short for a cyclops, but tall compared to the rest of us, and he's built like two trucks side-by-side. "But we don't mate. Not like... you guys do." He gives me a look of pity, and I hate it. "What are you supposed to do when your damn body picks someone who won't pick you?"

I don't say it aloud, but I know the answer. Probably die alone and miserable, always feeling like I'm missing a part of myself.

It's times like these I wish my dad was still alive, so I could ask him what I should do. I don't even know if I can tell my mother what I did at DreamTogether, much less that I've bonded with the human carrying my cub. She always wanted me to have a family, and I think this turn of events might break her heart.

"What are you going to do?" Caleb says after a while. "Anything?"

My shoulders sag helplessly. "What *can* I do? She made it clear where we stand." I wrap my hand around the cold beer and sink into the chill of it.

"Well, if it's meant to be, then she'll find her way back to you," he says. I just nod along, saying platitudes to end the conversation, hoping that he's right but knowing the chance is zero to none.

Just then, my phone buzzes.

It's Dee. I hurry to open the message so quickly that I almost drop my phone.

> Hey. So, there's an important appointment coming up. Twenty weeks. They're going to do an ultrasound, and should be able to tell us the sex.

I read the message once, then again, and then a third time just to make sure I understood it.

She's inviting me to her ultrasound. She's reaching out to me, offering to include me.

I fall over myself to respond right away.

> I would love to come. Date and time, and I'll be there.

I sound over-eager and needy, but I don't care. I'll do anything just to be near her, and this... this would be significant.

This is important to our cub's growth.

> It's Friday at one at the DreamTogether office.

She sounds very curt, but I don't mind. I'll take anything.

"Is that her?" Caleb asks as I assure her that I'll be there and put away my phone.

I nod. "It's something, at least. She's going to let me come to the checkup appointment."

Caleb slaps me on the back. "Here's your opportunity, then," he says. "Show her you can be better than what brought you here."

I don't know if that'll be enough, but I'll sure as fuck try.

When I get home, I run to my calendar, write down the appointment in huge, red letters, and then circle it a few times for good measure.

I get to see her again.

But I also have to remember that I can't expect more from her than this. She's allowing me in, and I shouldn't push for any more or I risk damaging it. I promise myself that on Friday, I'll be the most polite, completely platonic father I can be.

DEE

My insomnia is even worse these days. I stay up late watching re-runs of old shows, but I don't go for any late night walks anymore. Now I'm afraid of what might happen if Russ *isn't* there. At least my plants are doing well—flourishing, actually, growing bigger leaves and blooms than ever since I started fertilizing them.

But nothing chases away the aching underneath my skin, deep inside me. Now that I know Bill isn't just some stranger who fucked me better than I've ever been fucked in my life, but also a warm, kind doctor who works in a maternity ward and thinks about my emotional needs... it's even harder not to picture myself with him.

I can't offer what he wants. I can't be what he needs me to be, what his instincts are waiting for. I signed up to carry this baby and then give it away. I'm not cut out to care for one, to be someone's partner, to make a family with him.

This is all just a big mistake.

Still, I decide not to tell DreamTogether about what Russ has done. And when they send the reminder that it's time for the twenty-week appointment, my thoughts go straight to him.

He would want to know about this. And now that the seal of anonymity is broken, there's no reason not to include him in the proceedings regarding his child.

His child, I remind myself. That's why he should know. Especially if something of concern comes up, it would be better to have his say in how we manage it.

I want to send another message and tell him not to get any ideas, that this invitation is not about the two of us, only the well-being of his baby. I'm just not sure that's true.

The fluorescent lights in the doctor's office are really hurting my eyes. I've become much more sensitive to light lately, and it feels like yet another of those annoying little changes I've been experiencing as time goes on. Like right now, I have to pee again already.

I head off to the bathroom. The door's locked, so I wait and wait until it opens and a huge pregnant woman walks out. I see my future in her as she waddles over to a chair in the waiting room and sits down.

I'm not looking forward to it, but this is what I signed up for.

When I leave the bathroom a few minutes later, I find one very tall wolfman in a nice button-up and khaki pants peering around the room.

Russ. He's cleaned up impeccably, all of his brown fur

shiny and smooth. When his yellow eyes catch mine, they widen, and his long mouth curls into a smile.

"Dee." He takes two long, quick strides towards me, then abruptly stops a few steps away. I thought surely he was going to walk right up to me and wrap his arms around me.

If he did, would I have objected?

He scratches the back of his head. "It's good to see you," he says, staying where he is, and his gaze travels down from my face to my belly. His eyebrows tilt and he gets a shy look on his face, like he already adores a baby he hasn't even met yet.

"You, too," I say amiably. He's clearly trying to exercise respect and restraint, and I appreciate that. I head toward one of the chairs and sit, then pat the one next to me. Russ navigates himself into the chair meant to accommodate human women like me, and holds up his shoulders so he doesn't spill too far into my seat.

"How is, um, the cub?" he asks, tilting his head. Though his coat is well cared for, looking at him up close, there are bags under his eyes. He seems exhausted.

"Fine, I think. I guess we'll find out today." I absently stroke the slight swell of my belly. "It's going to be a while still, though."

His eyes follow my hand, and he swallows. "Yeah. Another five months."

It's going to be a really long five months. I sigh. "Yeah. And I'm only halfway through."

The hopefulness falls from his face at the tone of my voice. He looks down at his lap and pins his hands to his thighs, like he's trying not to do something else with them.

"Thank you for the invitation," he says at last, offering me a weak smile. "I'm really happy to be included."

"Well, it's your kid," I say, before thinking twice about it.

He cringes, then turns his head away and nods. "Right."

We wait like that for another five minutes, this time without speaking, until the nurse comes to get us. Then, once we're in the patient room, I'm instructed to take off my pants and lie down on the table in the stirrups until the doctor comes.

Russ is very considerate about not looking anywhere untoward, though, and turns away as I change, keeping his eyes on either my face or the doctor's.

I had to explain to DreamTogether a version of what happened—that Russ and I met out in the world, and we discovered, through supposed happenstance, that we'd been matched up. As a result, we requested that we both be a part of the process that typically I would have gone through alone.

I give the doctor a Cliff's notes version, but I'm not sure he believes us.

"Well, all right," he says, grabbing a bottle of lube. "If there's as good a time as any for the father to be involved, it's today."

While the doctor gets started inserting the ultrasound wand, I sense Russ tensing up. He's watching very intently, and when I cringe at the cold invasion, the wolfman gets a look on his face like he could murder.

I forgot that Russ is an OB/GYN, too. I wonder if this human doctor isn't as good at his job, though, and that's what's bothering him.

"Because this is technically considered a high-risk pregnancy, we're going to keep a close eye on this one." We all turn to the screen as the picture changes. I've seen this image before, but it's Russ's first time on the patient side, and his eyes are glued to the display as the doctor investigates my uterus. I cringe as he touches a few sensitive places.

"There," he says, pointing at the screen.

The fuzzy shape is the same as before, sort of like an oversized nut, but it's grown quite a bit. "Wow," I say. "It's a lot bigger."

Russ has a huge, wide grin on his face.

"Amazing," he says quietly, leaning forward to get a better look, which means he's right up against the edge of the table, his soft fur pressed to my bare skin. "We made that."

Dr. Hodgens glances at me, but Russ misses it.

"We did," I agree. I can't help but remember how we did it, too, on that bench in that sterile room. How he licked me all over, then fucked me the best I've ever been fucked in my life.

Russ's nostrils flare, and his head snaps over to look at me.

"Things will progress much more quickly from here," the doctor says as he continues his scan. "We'll need to increase your vitamin intake. And your blood work scores were low last time. Are you eating enough?"

Great. Of course I haven't been eating enough. I've been stressed out and unhappy.

"I'm trying, but I think I'm just naturally low," I hedge. It doesn't look like Russ believes it, though.

The doctor nods. "Then we'll move you up to a bigger supplement."

"There," Russ suddenly interrupts, peering at the screen. "If it were a male cub, that would be..." He squints. "Nope, I don't think so."

"It is most likely a female," the doctor agrees. "Good eye."

"Russ does this for a living," I say. "So I would hope so."

The hint of a smile pulls at Russ's mouth, and he gives me an appreciative nod.

The rest of the appointment is uneventful, and neither the doctor, nor Russ, discovers anything wrong.

"It's always hard to know with monster-human hybrids," Dr. Hodgens says as he withdraws the wand. "Every pregnancy is different. But I do know most of the warning signs to watch out for, and I think the two of you are good to go with a healthy baby." He glances sideways at Russ. "Or, um, cub."

With that, the doctor cleans off the wand and steps out of the room so I can get dressed. Russ carefully keeps his eyes turned away, but I can tell his mind is somewhere else.

"Are you okay?" I ask as I pull on my jeans.

He glances at me, then realizes I haven't quite zipped up and hastily looks away. "Y-yeah. I'm fine." I can tell his claws are extended, though, and his fur on his neck is bunched up. I think about asking more questions, but do I really want to know the answers?

Instead, I finish up, and we exit the office together. In the parking lot, though, Russ hesitates.

"Can I... come to the next one, too?" he asks, hovering before stepping off the curb.

I pause. "In two weeks?" He nods quickly. "Sure. I don't see why not."

Relief passes over his face. "Thank you, Dee." He bites his lower lip. "Really. For letting me be involved."

"Like I said," I say, unlocking the car, "it's your kid."

All the hope drains out of Russ's face. "Right. Well, see you in two weeks." He heads off into the parking lot without another word.

twenty

RUSS

I HATED WATCHING that man touch Dee. On a basic, intellectual level, I knew I had nothing to worry about. But on that other level, the one I'm trying desperately to banish, I wanted to eat him. Not to mention that he was sloppy with the wand, which made it far more uncomfortable than necessary for Dee.

But I'll get to see her again in two weeks. At least while I'm sitting in the room with my mate and cub, alone for a few minutes... my instincts grew quieter, and I felt a brief, momentary peace.

Except that as the days to the next appointment drag on, the need rises up inside me again. This isn't enough, but it's all I'm going to get.

My life becomes a cycle of worrying about Dee living at her apartment alone, going to the gym, going to work, eating somewhere in between, worrying about Dee, and then going to sleep. I repeat the cycle every day, wishing I just knew where she was, what she was doing, whether or not she was eating right.

I know she was lying to the doctor, and that she hasn't been taking care of herself. I didn't watch her all that time for nothing. The only thing she eats before 11 a.m. is cereal, and then after that she makes tea, before walking her dog and then settling in for an evening of salad and chicken fingers, or sometimes she orders pizza.

She orders pizza a lot more often than she probably should.

To sate my growing restlessness, I go hunting again, and now I've gone twice as often in one month as I have in the last three years. It curbs the need enough that I can clear my head and wait patiently until the following Friday, when it's time for Dee's next checkup.

I take care with my appearance, hoping it doesn't look like I tried too hard, then drive in so I arrive two minutes before our scheduled time.

Dee is polite again, and I wonder if this is my destiny. To be an acquaintance to my mate, my cub's mother. I wonder what I can possibly do to show her that I'm right for her.

It is a marvel, even a second time, to see our cub up on the ultrasound screen. There she is. My chest swells as I look at her, and then down at Dee. She's also too busy staring at the screen to notice me watching her, observing her, studying all the lovely planes of her face. Her breasts are slowly growing, which I can only tell because I haven't seen her for two weeks.

My heart aches thinking of the wet nurse waiting to step in as soon as the cub is born. What will my life be like, raising this little one by myself? That had been my plan all along, and I had loved the idea of it—loved it enough that I saved and saved so I could afford the package at Dream-Together.

And now... the thought of Dee walking out of our lives makes the clamp around my heart constrict so tight, I think my lungs might burst.

"She's beautiful," I say. Dee nods in agreement, but doesn't speak. When I look down at her, her eyes are shimmering. Then she looks away from the screen and covers up her chest with her arms, and she's quiet for the rest of our time with the doctor.

After the appointment, I pause outside the DreamTogether office building, just like last time. I can't let her leave without finding out what she was thinking about.

"Are you all right?" I'm the one who asks this time.

"What do you mean? I'm fine." She winces. "He's sure not gentle with that thing, though."

"He fucking sucks at it," I say.

A laugh bursts out of her. She wipes at one of her eyes, and it's clear she was on the verge of tears.

"What's wrong?" I ask. "Really. You seemed upset in there."

Dee furrows her brow. "Nothing's wrong," she says, her voice a tad defensive. "Just pregnancy hormones."

"Hormones or not, your feelings still matter," I say. "I just want to make sure that you're all right, Dee. Is Robbie..." His name comes out of my mouth like a curse, because I don't even want to acknowledge that someone else is tending to her needs. "...is he taking good care of you?"

And just like that, her eyes well up with tears again, and this time they all burst free.

"No!" she cries, rubbing her eyes and trying to whisk them away.

"No?" I feel my lips curl to expose all of my fangs. "Has he done something to you? I'll—"

"I dumped him, okay?" she says through what have quickly become sobs. "So no. Robbie is not *taking care of me*."

I blanch. She left the human man? "Why?" I ask rather stupidly. I should be over the moon, but I want to know why she's crying when she's the one who dumped him.

"Because I fucked you, that's why!" She collapses against her car, using the hood to hold herself up. Someone stares at us as they walk from the parking lot up to the front door of the building. That's how she sees it. And, I suppose, *fucking* is what we did out in the woods that day.

"It wasn't right to stay in a relationship with him after screwing him over like that," she says between sniffles.

I want to be pleased that Robbie is now done and over with, but I can tell that it hurts Dee immensely.

"Would you..." I begin slowly. "Would you like an iced coffee?" We're reaching the tail end of summer now, but it's still quite hot out today. "I can just listen. I know that without him, you're home alone a lot."

She frowns at this reminder that I watched her when I shouldn't have, but I'm not going to pretend it didn't happen.

"Yeah," she admits through her tears, sniffling. "I am. Even with Boomer around, it's not the same."

I nod in understanding. I've lived alone for a long time, but I'm always socializing with the other staff at the hospital. Now Dee is home alone all day when her friends are at work, and they can't meet with her every single night of the week. She went out of her way to adopt Boomer. There's something in her life she wants, but doesn't have yet.

"We'll just talk, okay?" I say, opening the passenger door of my car for her. As if on autopilot, the weeping Dee steps in, then I close it behind her.

I drive us both carefully over to the same coffee spot as the last two times we met. She laughs through her tears as we pull in.

"You really like this place. We were in a totally different part of town and now you'll have to take me back to get my car."

I shrug. "Worth it for the croissants here."

When we get our drinks, we sit outside, and at last Dee's crying has abated. Her face is an adorable flushed pink, though her eyes are still red. I wait for her to speak first, so I don't crowd her.

"Russ," she says finally after a few minutes of silence. "What do you really want?"

I turn and blink at her. The words that almost come out of my mouth are, *you*. But I don't want to come on so strong.

"What do you mean by 'want'?" I ask. "I want a more peaceful world. I want food to cost less. I want people to be healthy."

She shakes her head. "For yourself. Why did you do DreamTogether in the first place?"

Oh. I stare at her for a moment, trying to remember what I came into this hoping to achieve, because what I've found in the meantime is so far beyond what I imagined.

"A family," I say finally. "I've seen so many people find joy in it. I've probably wanted a cub of my own since I was... well, a cub myself. I want a child to play games with, to watch them grow, to teach them sports and help them go into the world on their own and spread their wings. And to know that I was a part of it."

Dee is watching me, not speaking, as I finish. Her lips are slightly parted, and her brows are drawn together in sympathy.

"That's the whole reason?" she asks. "Nothing like carrying on your family name or whatever?"

I furrow my brow in confusion. "What? No." I sigh and lean my head on my hand, elbow propped on the table. "My parents were... fine. I came out all right. But that's not why. I want to be there for all the firsts. I can't wait to teach her how to hunt, and see the first time she tastes fresh prey. I want to be there when she gets her first good grades, and when she gets her first pet. I want to teach her how to swim." Dee arches an eyebrow. "Swimming is an important skill," I say, holding up one clawed finger. "You never know when you might fall in a river."

She laughs at this, and it feels so good to make her laugh after watching her cry. "I never thought to be prepared for surprise rivers."

Her hand is lying out on the table, and I want so badly just to scoop it up in mine. Instead, I touch just the pad of my finger to her palm, dwarfing it, and her eyes dart up to mine.

"What did *you* want?" I ask her. "When you did Dream-Together?"

It doesn't look like she expected this question, and I wonder if even she knows the answer to it.

"A job," she says, her tone carefully neutral. "That's all."

More and more, I think this is what she's been telling herself all along, and now she believes it. I want to ask her if she felt anything today while we looked at the ultrasound of our cub together, but I know that would be crossing a line.

"And what do you want now?" I ask, pushing just a little harder. I know her. I understand her, I believe. She longs for connection, just as I do, and that was certainly why we bonded so quickly and so easily. She's a caretaking type, like

I am, and that much is apparent just in how she loves Boomer.

And I think trying to put up a wall between us, between herself and our cub, is taxing Dee to her limit.

"I don't know," she finally says, lowering her eyes. "I really don't. I just... I know that I'm sad all the time, Russ."

The way she says my name, but in such a melancholy voice, makes me want to put my arms around her and drag her into my lap. I want to take her back to my house and tuck her in a blanket with hot cocoa and a movie, then snuggle her until she falls asleep.

"Were you sad when you were with Robbie?" I ask, trying to use my gentlest voice.

She shakes her head. "It was more like... before, I could hide the sad underneath where Robbie was. Now there's nowhere for it to go."

"And Boomer isn't enough?"

"He's wonderful," Dee says, and the tears are coming back. "But no, he's not enough." She sniffles. "I thought this job would be great, Russ. I thought it would be exactly what I needed." The tears are streaming faster now, and people are looking at us, but I couldn't care less about them even if the world was ending. I lean closer to Dee and gently stroke her back. "Instead, I feel more alone than ever. Except for this one." She slides her hand off the table, and onto her belly. I bite my lip because I want nothing more than to encompass her hand in mine.

"Are you worried that when it's over, you'll be alone again?" I ask.

She nods her head as she cries. I can't help it anymore, and I reach around her to gather her up in my arms. She doesn't resist at all, and starts crying harder into the fur of my chest.

"You don't have to be alone," I tell her quietly, so no one can overhear. I rock her gently from side to side. "It's okay to want more. To ask for more."

Dee hiccups. "But I don't want the same thing you want, Russ. I would never make a good mom. And I'm really not a good choice for a 'mate,' either."

I pull back and peer down my nose at her, perplexed. "What? Of course you are. You're..." *Don't come on too strong*, I try to tell myself. Though I don't know if I have a choice but to say what I feel right now. "You're perfect, Dee. You're everything that I..." I trail off. I've spent my whole life wanting her, almost four decades of it. It was fully worth the wait.

"That you, what?" she asks, and I can't lie to those huge, blue eyes.

"You're all I could have hoped for, everything I could have dreamed of," I finally tell her. "You're funny and sassy, and you love so deeply. I see how you care about Boomer, how he means the world to you. You treasure things closely."

I let one of my hands settle on hers where it rests atop her belly, and splay my fingers. "You would make an amazing mom."

She sniffs a few more times, but her tears have slowed.

"I don't know you," she says after a time. "I don't know the real Russ at all. So what am I supposed to say to that?"

I can't help but smile. She thinks this is such a bad thing.

"Then why don't we get to know each other?" I ask, letting her go now that she's calmer.

"Oh." It's like the thought never occurred to Dee. "Yeah. I guess... I guess I would like that."

twenty-one

DEE

I THINK I just agreed to go on a date with Russ.

His whole face lights up, those furry eyebrows rising high on his forehead. His lips pull back from his white fangs as he smiles.

"You would?" he asks, radiant. "Do you want to get dinner with me?"

"Tonight?" I ask. "Don't you have work?"

He waves a hand. "Dr. Owens owes me a favor." His face grows more serious. "Dee, after today, after seeing our cub up on that screen... I want to be a part of your life in any way I can, now, during, and after. In whatever capacity you can handle."

His words are so honest and freely-given that I'm not sure I deserve them.

"Russ," I begin.

"Before you come up with reasons to say 'no,' just know there aren't any expectations from me. All I want is your company."

He may not have expectations, but that doesn't mean I don't. If we're alone together anywhere along the way, I know what both our bodies will want.

Gently, Russ drops a hand on my shoulder. "I'm happy just being near you," he says. "That's all. Nothing more, okay?"

I don't tell him, *but what if I want more?* Instead, I agree to a time and place, and then Russ gives me a ride back to my car. He plays nineties rock that makes me notice the speckle of gray appearing on his muzzle fur, and I think how utterly, drop-dead handsome he is.

A sweet guy with a good job, who's amazing in bed, and even has lovely marks of maturity like that... I'm a goner.

Dinner goes by in a flash of light. We have Italian food, which is, apparently, Russ's favorite, at a restaurant in Dunsville, where he actually lives. It's a majority monster city, where all the chairs are sized for guests much larger than I am.

"Oops," Russ says. "I guess I should have asked for a high chair."

I snort into my water, and it jumps out of the cup. We both laugh, and that's how the rest of our meal goes: laughing, joking, talking a little about our childhoods. My parents liked to go out a lot and see their friends, which meant most of the time I cooked my own meals, which eventually became me eating cereal for dinner every day.

"So that's why you're all about cereal," he says, and sometimes I forget how he watched me through my window for weeks.

"It's just easier," I say defensively.

He holds up both hands. "I'm not much of a cook myself."

"So who's going to feed the kid?" I say, half-joking. But Russ's face turns serious.

"I have cooking classes lined up, for when she's weaned. I want to make my own baby food."

I blink. He has a whole plan already.

"How are you going to, you know..." I gesture vaguely at my boobs. "Feed her?"

For a moment, his eyes search mine, and then he nods his head and looks away. "I have a professional booked," he says, stabbing the remnants of his spaghetti with a fork.

He's got that figured out, too.

"This must have cost you a lot of money," I say quietly. And the part I don't say out loud: it must also mean the world to him to have a baby of his own.

"Money doesn't buy happiness, but it can sure get us close," he says with a wry smile. His bright amber eyes rise back up to mine. "I've been saving for a long time, and this will probably finish cleaning me out. But it's more than worth it."

Wow. Having a family means this much to him.

When dinner's over, I find I don't want to leave because I've been having such a good time. Russ had a childhood somewhat like mine, where he spent more time taking care of himself than his parents did. He watched out for his little brother, too, and didn't get to be a young boy for as long as maybe he should have.

But he doesn't resent it. He wants to give his own child a different kind of life, and that's part of what drives him.

It's fucking hot.

I choose to be better than my base instincts, though, and

when we've paid the check, I go back out to my car. Russ nods in understanding.

"Can we do this again soon?" he asks, playing absently with his fob.

"Sure."

"Lunch, before I go to work tomorrow?"

Tomorrow? So soon?

Ugh, that sounds great. Too great. I could see him again in less than twenty-four hours?

"I understand if you want more time than that," he says, like he can read right off my soul.

"No, it's fine." Fuck it. Like Liesel said, I should do what I want, not what I feel like I'm supposed to do. And what I want is to see Russ again as soon as possible. "I can meet tomorrow."

"Great. I'll see you then."

He grins like a little kid as he gets into his car and drives away.

RUSS

I'm probably pushing her too hard, but I can't help myself. Every moment I'm near her is like walking out into the sun on a dark, cold day.

The following afternoon I pick Dee up at her house, and invite Boomer along to have lunch at my place. I know it's a rather personal thing to ask for at this stage, but she agrees anyway.

Dee bolts upright in the car as we approach the gate. "Wait. This is where you live?"

I nod as I enter a code on the gate and it opens. "I wanted to cook for you myself. I actually can do it, they're just not... kid-friendly recipes."

Dee quirks an eyebrow at me as we drive in. She peers out the window.

"Dude," she says. "You desperately need to mow your lawn."

I sigh and open the garage door. "I know. It's been low on my list."

She gets a look in her eye like she could see herself getting behind a lawn mower. "Do you like yard work?" I ask.

"If I had a yard, I would." She mimics snipping. "I've always wanted to be that guy who trims hedges into cool shapes. You have lots of hedges."

"Trim all the cool shapes you want," I tell her. "The HOA complains enough already, what's one more thing?"

She gets a giddy look on her face like she might take me up on my offer. I hope she does. She has a knack for plants, just like she has a knack for nurturing everything in her life.

Once inside the house, I drop my keys by the front door and usher Dee in behind me.

"Bathroom?" she asks immediately, and I wonder how long she's been holding out.

"Down there, on the right," I say, pointing to the hall. She nods and jogs away like the need has become pretty urgent.

While she's gone, I set out some orange juice and iced tea, then get started on the salad. I sear quartered figs, then pull out the stovetop grill to cook some chicken breast I marinated overnight just for this. When Dee comes back, she seats herself at the kitchen island so she can watch me cook.

I do my best to put on a good show. I want her to see that I can handle things, that she wouldn't be stuck cooking and cleaning if she took me up on my offer. If only she knew how much cleaning I'd done last night just to get this place presentable.

"You have a nice house," she says offhandedly while she eats. She studies the open living room next to the kitchen, where we're sitting at the small dining table by the front windows. "Doctor money, huh?"

In the middle of a laugh, I choke on my food. She throws me a worried look and gets up like she might try to give me the Heimlich maneuver, but I wave her off and swallow down the lettuce stuck in my throat.

"Man, sorry, that was a dick thing to say." Dee rubs the back of her head. "Since you're basically paying my salary."

I thump my chest, shaking my head. "No, no. You're right. It's the only reason I could even consider DreamTogether." I slug back some water. "And I don't mind that it goes to you. To my cub."

Maybe I shouldn't have said that last part, because her eyes darken a little, and she looks away at an abstract, green painting on the wall. Then she takes another bite of her food, and hums with pleasure.

"Yeah, okay, I see what you mean by not kid friendly," she says, speaking around her chicken. "This is fucking delicious, though."

I swell with pride, knowing I could present her with a salad in a way she actually enjoys.

"Will you eat this instead of cereal?" I ask.

"Any day you want."

But she looks even more thoughtful now, her brows drawn together tight as she finishes her meal. I wonder where she's gone in her mind, because so far, I thought things were going well.

"Do you want to see?" I ask her as she drinks the last drop of her tea, then sighs and pats her belly.

"See what?" Dee asks.

"The nursery."

Her eyes grow round, and then a look crosses her face I can't quite read. Did I make a mistake by asking?

"Sure," she says suddenly, standing. "Show me."

I get to my feet and lead her up the stairs to the second floor. Here there's a railing that overlooks the big open floor plan downstairs.

"Don't worry," I say when she peers over the side. "I got a special fence to put across it, so she can't slip through."

I hear Dee exhale, and smile to myself as I lead her down the hall, away from my bedroom.

I bought a place with four rooms, I'm still not sure why. One is my home office, which I use rarely. One is the nursery, and one is a guest room that also never gets any traffic.

Then there's the master bedroom that maybe someday, I'll get to show her, too.

Take it slow, at her speed, I tell myself.

I open the first door on the left, and step aside to let Dee through. But the moment she's inside, she gasps and freezes in the doorway.

I started decorating the nursery before DreamTogether had even accepted me, just out of hope. Once I was on the books, though, I went wild picking out everything I wanted for it. The wallpaper is cream-yellow with playful, swirling designs, perfect for baby eyes searching out new shapes. I hung a mobile over the crib, which I painted white myself with yellow accents. The changing table matches, and baskets of stuffed animals hang from the ceiling in the corners. There's a reading nook with gossamer curtains, where I imagined myself sitting with my cub in my lap, teaching them how to sound out words in a picture book.

Suddenly, I hear Dee crying, and my head jerks toward her in alarm. I can't see her face from where I'm standing behind her.

"Dee?" I ask, running a hand down her back. "Are you—"

"It's so cute," she whimpers, wiping her face. "Do you have any idea how... how sweet and wonderful this is? And you're all prepared to do it by yourself."

"That was the plan," I say hesitantly. *Before you*, I want to add.

She just nods, still crying. "Fucking hormones," she grumbles, wiping more tears away.

"We can leave, if you want." I walk back out into the hall, but Dee shakes her head. She turns around to face me and her eyes are red, her cheeks stained with tracks of pink. All I want to do is hold her until those tears stop.

"Look," she says, rather brusquely. "I'm not going to promise you I'm going to be anyone's mom. I don't know if I'm ready for that."

I can completely understand this. It's not what she signed up to do.

"I don't expect you to promise anything," I say.

"Shush." She waves a hand at me, still wiping snot from her nose. "But I should say that I find you... insanely, wonderfully, blissfully hot. Like every smoke alarm in this house is going off."

I tilt my head, because I don't hear anything, but then realize she's making a joke.

She still likes me.

"Thank you," is all I can think of to say, and she smiles warmly. Then she takes a step closer, and another one, and now that she's in my bubble and her smell is so delightfully close, all I want is to touch her.

So, boldly, I do. I let my hand come to a rest on her waist, and Dee gives a small nod of approval.

I think now I know what she was trying to say. She wants me, but she's not ready for more. She's not ready for the future I'm picturing, with the two of us working together to raise our cub.

But as long as I can have her in any capacity, I am more than happy.

twenty-two

DEE

RUSS'S BEDROOM is as beautiful as the rest of his house. It's nothing too ritzy, but the furnishings are minimalist, the appliances are stainless steel, and there are windows *everywhere*. The place is just full of natural light, and I know I would love living here.

I can't picture that kind of thing, though. There are too many implications. What I can picture, however, is how Russ is going to look without any of his clothes on.

He lowers his eyebrows as I study him, and a wicked grin reveals all his teeth. He encircles me with his arms, drawing me over the threshold into the big, open room. Right in the middle is the biggest bed I've ever seen, with a blue comforter and blue sheets that match the curtains.

In silence, we each shed our clothes one article at a time. This isn't going to be some wild fuck in the woods. When I'm naked, I sit down on the bed, and he kneels in front of me so he's just slightly tipping his head to look up at me. His cold nose brushes mine, and then his lips graze my mouth.

The way he kissed me when we fucked, his tongue down my throat, is very different from what he's doing now—sampling my lips with his own, which are surprisingly dexterous for the shape of his snout, and then gently sucking. My mouth opens of its own accord, and his tongue darts out, tracing the edge of my lips before sliding through.

Instantly my body warms at the memory of when we last did this, and I hear Russ's breath speed up. He shudders under my hands, and his grip on my hips tightens.

"I'm doing it differently this time," he says against my mouth, and his eyes are intense. With that, he pulls away from me, and then spreads my legs with one huge paw. His shoulders curl as he bends down, and I'm fully exposed to him.

He doesn't go straight between my thighs, though. No, Russ drags his tongue down from my lips to my neck, where he circles right at the hollow of my throat. Finally, he loops it around one of my nipples, and then brings his mouth down to nibble on it.

"Oh, fuck," I say, because I didn't realize how sensitive they'd become. He pauses, but I sling my hands around behind his ears and pull him towards me again. With a chuckle, he puts his whole mouth on it this time, sucking it in between his lips and grazing it with just the very tips of his teeth. I squirm, and he lets out a satisfied sigh, like just that taste brought him immense satisfaction.

He repeats his assault on my other nipple, and gently cups both my breasts in his huge paws, the tips of his claws tickling my flesh.

"These are amazing," he says, fondling them with the utmost gentleness before letting them go. Then his hands travel down to my belly, which is even rounder now than it was the last time we did this. The lust in his eyes softens, and he traces the curve with one claw before leaning down to press a kiss to it.

"Can I?" he asks, rubbing his ear.

I nod, even though I thought we were about to have sex. "Sure."

He gently leans the side of his head against my belly, cradling the swell with his other hand. His eyes close, and his tail, which had been sticking straight out, slowly lowers to the ground.

"I can hear her heart," he says in a quiet voice. I almost can't make out the words. "It's so fast."

"Because she's still small," I tell him, stroking the fur of his head. Russ lets out a breath and wraps his other arm around me from behind, nuzzling my belly with his cheek.

That's when, for the first time, she *kicks*.

"Whoa," Russ says, pulling away. We exchange shocked looks. "Has that ever happened before?"

"No!" I'm a little stunned myself by how surprising it felt. "Never."

He smiles broadly. "Maybe she knows when her mother is getting excited." He continues licking and kissing his way down my belly, underneath it to where my legs are still spread wide for him. His sweet smile turns into a much more mischievous smirk as he surveys me there.

"Such a beautiful, furry pussy," he hums, just as his tongue darts out to lick me. A shock travels through my body, so he does it again, and again I shiver all over. His licks grow faster, his tongue pressing down harder, and I wriggle as I moan.

Then he's on me like a predator, claws digging into the comforter as he goes wild with his mouth, licking every part of me, sliding his tongue inside me like he did when we first met and pressing it against my inner wall, where he strokes it up and down. My body is even more sensitive than before, and it's so good that it isn't long before I break. For only the third time in my life, that hot liquid streams out of me, and Russ lets out a lustful groan. He licks my oversensitive clit, trying to grab up everything I'm giving him.

Fuck. That's so hot. I can't stand it.

"Russ," I whimper, toppling back to the bed.

He climbs up and brackets my head with his arms. "What is it?" he asks, concerned. "The cub—?"

"No, no." I run a hand up his neck, behind his ear, then down his cheek and snout. "I just... please, fuck me."

A huge grin takes over his face, and he reaches down to palm his big, wet cock, which has long extruded from his furry sheath.

"Most happily," he says. "And I'm going to take you while looking at you, too."

He slides me up the bed so he can kneel between my legs, where he focuses intently on his task. I still can't fathom how something that size fits inside me, but when the soft, pointed head slides in, I have to accept that it does.

And oh, how well it does.

Russ groans as he buries himself just a quarter deep, then pauses to look down at me.

"Is that all right?" he asks. "Is anything painful or uncomfortable?"

I glare at him. "What are you talking about? You feel amazing. Please." I hook my heels into his ass, right at the base of his tail, and Russ buckles forward. Then I squeeze him inside me, and he whimpers. "More."

Rising up above me, he grabs my thighs with both clawed paws and shoves his cock deeper. Oh, there we are. That's him again—and this is where he belongs.

With me.

RUSS

There is no bliss like being buried inside your mate's cunt.

I thrust gently, shallowly, making sure not to go too deep until I know she's opened enough for me. But Dee gets frustrated with me quickly.

"Russ," she says, burying one hand in my scruff. "Do it like you mean it."

The primal, ravenous energy I've been trying to hold back rolls out of me, all at once. I reel my hips back and then plunge into her, sinking my cock in her heavenly body. She welcomes me with a cry, and it's most certainly a cry of pleasure.

She's so warm, so fucking wet, and with every stroke her channel flutters around me. My Dee feels like complete and utter heaven.

The harder I thrust inside of her, the more her belly jiggles and her swollen breasts bounce. I'm entranced by her, how her mouth falls open and her eyes go wide as I sheath myself even more fully inside her. It isn't long before I'm deep enough that my knot is teasing where it wants to be.

"Russ!" she cries, and I'm so happy it's my name, my *real* name this time.

"Tell me what you want," I say, lowering my snout to her ear and licking the shell of it.

"M-m-more." She cries out louder when I sink even further into her, as the flared edge of my knot starts to spread the lips of her pussy apart. "I want even more wolfman cock!"

Oh, my woman knows exactly what to say to me. I will

fuck her better than that human man could ever dream of. I will make love to her, and show her exactly what she means to me.

"Yeah?" I crouch down lower, hovering with my nose just barely touching hers as I pump harder with my hips. "You want this? All of it?" I pick her up by the hips and lift them up off the bed so I can get an even better angle, and then I push even more of my knot into her—taunting her, teasing her.

I'm really the one being taunted and teased. The thought of myself completely buried in her, her belly swollen full of my cub, has me so close to my release that I'm doing breathing exercises to hold it back.

"Yes, I want all of it!" She moans and sobs for me as I pump my hips faster, and I'm glad I have carpet this time so my claws can hook in as I drive into her, forcing her pink, swollen pussy to open wider and wider for me. Soon she's not moaning but crying out, her fingers buried in my fur like claws. There's nothing in the world that compares to this, my body singing to hers and hers singing back, a memory and a reflection of that very first time I walked into that sterile room and saw her waiting for me.

Dee drags me down close to her as my cock makes a wet *squelch* with each pass through her. But I haven't fucked her in some time, and her small body is struggling to take all of me. She's quivering, so close to her climax, mewling and crying my name, but I can't let her tip over yet. I'm going to savor her, worship her, and remind her why she's mine—and I'm hers.

Instead of pushing harder, I slow down my pace and swirl my cock around inside her, opening her even more for me. She moans and bucks, frantic for me to thrust again, so I push my knot in as far as it will go and then draw it out, until

Dee is writhing and whining and clutching me tight with her iron thighs.

"Russ!" she demands, and I feel her belly press into my own when she drags me down closer to her, using the sensitive flesh behind my ears. She looks into my eyes, and presses a kiss to my snout.

I take the opportunity to kiss her back, sliding my tongue into her mouth, before I finally shove my knot all the way inside her.

There's an audible *pop!* as it fits in, and Dee lets out a cry. I pull it free and then thrust it into her again, over and over, and now she's screaming my name.

Just to really torment her, I drop one hand down between us, where my knot has spread the lips of her pussy impossibly wide, and run just the tip of my claw over her clit. Dee is now thrashing underneath me, so I curl my finger and rub her with my knuckle, the way she likes, and she cries out again as I stuff my knot into her.

I make love to her like this, hard and slow, dragging my cock out and then squeezing it back in, until I'm so close to the edge that I have vertigo. I pull my tongue free of her mouth and murmur, "I'm going to stuff that pretty human pussy so full of me."

"You already put a cub in me," she says, her voice slurring with how drunk she is on my knot. I shove it into her again, and her head falls back in bliss. I want to tell her how I already want to fuck another one into her, but I need to be careful.

"And what a beautiful cub it will be." I nuzzle her face as I thrust into her faster, and her cries ratchet up in volume until she's filling the whole house with the sound of her pleasure. My little human, the love of my life, the mother of my cub and the meaning of everything.

I rub Dee harder, and all at once her tight channel clenches tight as a vise, and her scream is ear-piercing. I gasp, unable to hold back any longer as she starts to milk my cock for everything it's worth.

I slip my knot inside her, and when she squeezes down around it, I burst with a feral roar.

twenty-three

DEE

IT TAKES some time for the clouds to clear from our frantic lovemaking, and then even longer for Russ's swelling to come down enough that he can slip out of me again. Warm come rushes down my thigh, onto the comforter. I can already taste the edges of dreams as Russ lies down next to me, curling his huge, furry body around mine. He rests his hand on my belly and rubs it gently, like a crystal ball.

"Have you ever seen a half-human wolfperson?" I ask. I've wondered for some time how our baby might come out.

"I was friends with one growing up." He nestles his chin on top of my head. "He was a good guy. A little short."

I laugh.

"Most half-human hybrids come out looking like their monster parent," Russ says after a while in a more serious tone. I wonder if this is how he sounds when he's acting like a doctor. What would it be like to be his patient? *Probably would have a painful crush on him.*

"So our baby will look more like you?"

He nods. "Probably. Most likely."

I think about this for a while, and find that my hand has been absently stroking over his for some time. I'm starting to fall asleep in the warm afternoon light coming in the windows when I hear Russ's voice. "I have to go to work soon," he says, but when I move to get up, he keeps me lying down on the bed. "No, no. You and Boomer can stay here as long as you want. I have another car if you decide you want to go home."

He kisses my forehead, then covers me with the blanket and starts busying about putting his clothes back on. Soon, I've drifted off, and when I wake up, it's dark out and Boomer is lying on the bed next to me.

"Well, you made yourself right at home, didn't you?" I ask him, and he just lets out a little huff. I pet his head a few times before finally getting up.

There's a note on the kitchen table with a set of keys on top, but I'm not in any rush really. I just slept all day, and I feel like there isn't an ounce of tension in my whole body after the way Russ treated me like a queen earlier.

After finding some unseasoned, cooked chicken to feed to Boomer—which Russ thoughtfully left behind—I sit down on the couch and watch a television show. Later I dig out some leftovers, and before I know it, I've fallen asleep again.

Faint light is coming in the window when I hear Russ say, "I'm so happy to see you, my dear." He scoops me up and carries me back to his bedroom, where we curl up under the blankets together to sleep until noon.

RUSS

She fits rather perfectly into my life.

But I don't tell her that. I don't even imply that, letting her instead come to that conclusion on her own when we both awaken in the early afternoon, and we decide I ought to take her and Boomer home.

Now that the door has been opened, though, there is no closing it again. We see each other every other day, saving time for our friends in between. I invite her along to the next barbecue, even though the weather's turning colder, and Caleb offers her some flavored seltzer because he knew she was coming. I have one, too, and I think not drinking has actually been good for me.

The cub has grown again at our next appointment, though I knew that already from watching and listening to my mate's soft body every day. During this exam, Dee holds my hand tight to hers, and we all jump when the cub kicks inside her.

"A very active one," Dr. Hodgens says, noting our linked hands with a twitch of his mouth. "Must have some eager parents."

A little of Dee's smile falls, because I'm still not sure that she's ready.

She's now over at my home more days than she's not, but I haven't yet extended an invitation to move in. I'm taking things at her speed, waiting for her cues. My favorite activity is to bring her up into my lap so she's using my body like a recliner, then wrap my arms around her while we watch a movie. Afterwards, perhaps during, I dip my claws into her pants and simply taste her with my fingers, spreading her open for me.

I've taken Dee all sorts of ways, to show her how good it

can be with me, every day for the rest of her life. She liked to ride me at first, but now her body is too heavy, and so I often fuck her underneath me.

"Doggy style," she'll say, gasping, as she turns over to get on her hands and knees and expose her perfect rear to me. "It's easier on my back."

Oh, how taking her this way reminds me of when I first sowed this cub in her, and I've torn some holes into my bed with how furiously I'm overtaken by the instinct to breed her full again.

But nothing compares to bringing her legs up over my hips, and watching her ever-growing belly bounce with each of my thrusts. I'm more careful when I give her my knot, but she doesn't seem to want my care. She always demands more.

"Russ?" Dee asks one night, while I'm still stuck inside her.

"Mm?" I love to bury my snout in her hair after I fuck her and breathe in deep, filling up my head with her ripe smell. The way her flavor sweetly hums my name, I know she was meant to be mine.

"It seems kind of silly that I'm paying for a whole separate apartment. Don't you think?"

I can't help the smile that spreads across my face. "It is silly," I agree. "Do you want to move in here? It won't require much change to your lifestyle, I don't think."

She giggle-snorts, which tightens her up around me, and I buckle forward. A rumble of pleasure fills my throat as Dee pushes her hips back against mine, bringing my swollen cock even further into her. My eyes roll back in my head as my overstimulated knot is squeezed and milked.

She knows just how to drive me absolutely wild.

"Boomer already knows this neighborhood better than

ours," Dee says, rhythmically rolling her hips so I groan with every pass. "And he loves having a yard."

I manage to think about the outside world long enough to remember how she mowed the other day, then picked up a pair of gardening gloves and started trimming back the hedges. I like that she already feels my home is hers.

Dee flexes the muscles of her pelvic floor, and I'm incredibly pleased that I got her that video on doing kegels to make birth easier.

"Then move in," I grunt. "Please. Come and live with me, Dee. And bring your plants, too."

"Since you asked nicely." She gasps as I thrust into her, harder, and now her pussy has softened enough for me that I can pull my knot out and work it into her again. "I would love to."

She's seven out of ten months pregnant when we sell off most of her furniture, or give it away to the next tenants. It's easy for me to do the heavy lifting, and soon she's settled in my home, sharing my big master bedroom with me like I've always dreamed.

We have Liesel over often, or meet her at the local burger joint, since Dee's cravings for red meat only get more and more intense. A symptom of carrying my cub, unfortunately, is that she's starting to want things a cub would want to eat.

"It's like carrying around the world's most wriggly basketball," Dee groans as she sits down on one of the benches. "She's always moving around and kicking."

Liesel looks indifferent, as she often does. "I've heard babies do this," she says. "At least it's not crying yet." I get the sense Liesel isn't much of a children person. She looks at me next. "So, what is the plan? Are you two going to get married before the baby comes?"

Dee blanches. "Married?" She shoots me a guilty look as she splutters. "We haven't talked about that yet."

I shrug. "I don't see any rush. The cub comes when the cub comes, and our relationship doesn't hinge on that."

Liesel's eyebrows go up, and Dee gives me a relieved smile. She's not there yet, and I won't rush her. I want her to come at her own speed.

"I see," is all Liesel says, but her eyes never leave me. "Are you going to nurse the baby, then?"

Again, things Dee and I haven't talked about. I get the sense her friend knows that, and is intentionally stirring up the hornet's nest.

"I-I don't know," Dee says, wrapping her arms around herself. "I'll be right there, so, probably yes."

I don't express the joy I feel inside. I just stroke her back and slowly, her arms release. Then she smiles up at me and takes my hand.

By the time she is eight months pregnant, though, there are fewer smiles and more groans of irritation. I work out her tight muscles as best I can, kneading her sore body with my knuckles, and get more muscle relaxant from the hospital. I buy all her favorite foods, and make sure she does her exercises, as much as she hates it. At night, I curl up around her when she's too cold, and turn on the fan when she's too hot.

It's only been nine months when her water breaks.

DEE

The moment I go into labor, I see a side of Russ I've never seen before. All his hair is standing on end, and his lips are curled in a snarl as he grabs his phone and starts making calls.

"No," he snaps at someone on the other end. "She's coming to my hospital. I don't care about DreamTogether. Our relationship with you is concluded." Then he slams the END CALL button and makes another one.

"I'm bringing in Dee right now," he says into the phone. He's counting on his wrist, when I feel another twinge in my abdomen, and he restarts the count. "Yes, they're fairly close together."

A decision is made, and Russ helps me up off the couch. I limp along behind him out to the car, and he drives like a wolf out of hell toward his hospital, giving me instructions on how to breathe as we get closer. I try to tell him that I'm still doing all right, but he's on a mission now.

They're waiting for me when we arrive, and I'm led to a private room. This is a hospital in a monster area, so most of the doctors, nurses and patients are various trolls, gargoyles, and even a fairy woman who keeps her wings tucked away in her scrubs.

Russ stays with me, coaching me as my contractions get closer and closer together. A nurse comes in, and they take some measurements, talking quietly about how my labor is progressing. It's strange but comforting to see Russ become his doctor-self. He's knowledgeable and firm, and frequently stops to explain each step of the process to me.

"This is going to be difficult," he says in a serious tone. "She's early. I'm not sure what's going on."

I'm surprised that I don't detect fear in his voice, simply

unyielding determination. I nod, trusting in him to take care of her.

Discomfort soon turns to pain, and I'm suddenly quite angry with my past self for ever signing up for DreamTogether. Surely past me knew that future me would have to suffer through this.

Bitch.

As the contractions get more intense, Russ disappears, and I grow worried when he doesn't come back right away. I can't do this without him. I need him, right here, with me. This is *our* baby, the one that we made together, that he told me we would raise together.

He promised me.

My breathing is coming faster and I'm about to call out for him, when a wolfman walks in dressed in scrubs, his face covered in a mask. I gasp with relief.

"Russ!" He pulls down his mask to kiss me on the forehead.

"They told me I shouldn't do this myself, but I don't trust anyone else with you," he says, nuzzling my hair. Then he replaces his mask, brushes his hand once more over mine, and takes up his place at the bottom of the bed.

My labor is long and arduous, and Russ has frequent exchanges with other doctors and nurses that I can't hear. His face grows more worried as the pain drags on, but I'm afraid to know what might be wrong, even as I'm dying to make sure my baby is all right.

Still, I trust Russ to handle it, to make sure she gets here safely.

"Okay, my dear," he says to me, gently rubbing my thigh while another nurse stands nearby, poised to act. "She's ready to come out. She might be a little tangled, so I need you to push hard and fast, okay?"

"That's what I said," I joke, and then cry out as another bolt of agony lances through me.

But I do it. I do what he tells me, and I scream and sob and he praises me every step of the way. Except... there's no sound, not when she should be crying.

"Cut it off now," I hear Russ snap, and someone works between my legs.

There's a gasp, and then more muttering, that tapers into a long, drawn-out silence.

My heart speeds up. She has to be all right. She's mine. She's my girl, my daughter, and I need to meet her. I need to hold her, and learn who she is, and watch her become the best version of herself.

I'm on the verge of tears when suddenly, a small wail fills the air.

She's here.

twenty-four

RUSS

AFTER SNIPPING off the umbilical cord wrapped around her neck, our cub opens her tiny mouth and breathes. I nearly collapse in my relief.

She's arrived. Just holding her small, furry body in my big hands, a joy I could never have predicted sweeps through me, almost taking me off my feet. I glance up at Dee, who's panting and sweaty, and marvel that we could have made such a wondrous thing together.

I bring our newborn to my mate's side and gently place the cub in her arms, to give them skin-on-skin contact. Then the nurse returns, and walks Dee through the process of latching.

Finally, we're allowed to rest.

I take off my mask and hair net, and toss it all aside so I can scoot closer to them. Our cub's mouth is wrapped around her mother's nipple, and her wet fur moves with every suck. Her tiny hands are balled up at her chest, her tail curled between her legs.

She's pristine.

She also doesn't cry very much, but premature offspring are often weaker, and I'm simply glad that she's doing well enough on her own to not need support. She can remain with us, where she belongs.

We spend the night there, and I lie next to Dee on the small hospital bed, curled around her. Even as she sleeps, I stroke her dark hair, simply enjoying the sight of her, the feel of her, the warmth of her.

My mate and my cub are at last with me, right where I can watch over them forever.

Finally, the next day, we're allowed to go home. Dee insists on holding the cub in her arms, though I try to explain the necessity of using a car seat. When we park the car in the garage and Dee gets out, she says, "You decorated a whole nursery for her, but I want her in our room."

I simply nod. "All right. I'll move the crib."

Dee smiles brightly, as much as she can for how tired she is, and carries Ania inside with her.

That was the name we decided on, out of the blue. We hadn't ever discussed names, because it always came too close to the edge of the question, *will you be her mother?*

But I think Dee has answered without realizing it.

Ania is a quiet cub, quieter than she should be, but it's a blessing when Dee is exhausted in the days following. When Ania cries at night, I get up to carry her around, and feed her from one of the bottles Dee has already pumped and put in the fridge. Then, when her crying has abated, I gently rest her back in her crib and crawl into bed with my mate, where I can curl my arms around her and draw her in close to my chest.

Mine. My only.

I do ask her to marry me.

Ania is eighteen months old, and Dee has, on our mutual agreement, stopped taking her birth control. I'm surprised she wants to do it again, but at the same time, I think I understand her. We've made one cub together and seen how beautiful of a creature she is, and watched her blossom already in our care. What if we made more? What if I found purchase inside Dee's body again, and it spun another incredible web of life made of both of us?

When Ania is asleep and I've finished up with the dishes, Dee grabs my hand in hers, stroking over my claw with her thumb.

"Hey," she says in a sensual voice, leaning closer to me. "Would you like to go upstairs?"

I smirk at how little subtlety she has. Winding my arm around her waist, I lean down to nip at the shell of her ear.

"Oh, you want some wolfman cock?" I ask her, sliding my hand down her hip to her ass, where I can already tell her body is getting warmer for me.

She gasps in delight at the reminder of our first time together, and reaches down to squeeze my tail. It pulls a groan from my throat, and sends a shiver straight down into my balls. She massages underneath where it slides through the back of my jeans, and I bare my teeth at just how badly I need her already.

"Yes," she finally says, standing up on her toes to rub her face in my scruff. "I want your wolfman cock, Russ."

As always, the sound of my real name on her tongue gives me a raging hard-on.

Then Dee turns and runs, jogging up the stairs ahead of me. Seeing her flee kindles the instinctual desire to chase, so I sprint behind her two steps at a time, and snatch her up in my arms on the landing. She squeals as I carry her down the hall to our bedroom, where Dee has replaced the dark blues with sweet yellows and oranges. There I toss her onto the comforter, then jump onto it, caging her in with my hands. I taste her lips, but I'm so eager, thinking about how ripe her womb is for me, that I can't help my tongue darting deep into her mouth. She moans, her hips snapping up into mine, as my body tells hers what it wants.

And she answers, squeezing my ass, ducking her fingers under the band of my jeans and fiddling with the button to get them off. But I pull them away and pin her arms down to the bed.

"Stay there," I tell her, and she nods rapidly in understanding. I remember how she was once spread out for me on the bench with her arms strapped down, and consider that perhaps we should get into light bondage so I can tie her up like that again and have my way with her.

Dee would love that.

First I lift the hem of her shirt with one claw, then hoist it up over her head. Her special nursing bra comes next, and then her rather large breasts are exposed to me. I groan just at the sight of them, how full they are and how well they feed my cub.

But I have important work to do. I tear my eyes away and pull down her loose linen pants next, revealing the belly now kissed by pink lines and creases. I didn't think I could possibly get any harder, but I do, looking at this evidence of how she carried Ania and made her.

Dee spreads her legs, clearly voicing where she wants me —but then I remember what I'm here to do.

Well, besides get her pregnant again.

I quickly hop off the bed, and Dee whines behind me. "Where are you going?"

After digging around in my underwear drawer, I return to the bed with something tucked behind my back. I wanted this moment to be a little more special, but I know that now is the right time. Dee is happy as Ania's mother, and we thrive as partners. I want to go into this next stage knowing that she's mine forever.

She sits up and cocks her head at me. "What could possibly be more important than fucking me right now?" she grumps.

"I promise, this is." I kneel down between her knees in front of the bed, and her blue eyes get even bigger as I pull out the tiny box.

"Russ...?" she asks, her lips pursed in a way that's supremely cute.

"Dee." I pop the box open, and she goes straight as a rod. Her eyes dart down to the tiny ring inside, then back up to my face, her mouth open. "I know it's been... quite the road to get here."

She nods, her eyes already getting wet.

"But I can't see my life without you," I continue. "I don't *want* to ever live without you. So will you please marry me? And be mine forever?"

She's frozen like that, and for a moment I think she's going to turn me down. But then she flings herself at me, completely naked, and wraps her arms around my neck. Her wet eyes rub against my cheek as she hugs me for all I'm worth.

"Yes, you big, silly wolfman," she says, bringing in my snout to kiss the bridge of it, as she enjoys doing. "Let's get married."

My paw shakes as I slip the ring onto her slender ring

finger, and the jewel glints under the moonlight coming in the window. Then I sweep her up into my arms, encompassing her whole body, reveling in the knowledge that she's mine just as much as I am hers.

"Now take off your damn clothes," she says, and I bark a laugh.

Once she's spread out in front of me, I strip off everything, until it's just my fur and her skin. I'm about to descend on her like the animal I am, when she puts a hand on my chest, pushing me back into a crouch, my cock pointing toward her.

"Someone needs attention," she says mildly, licking her lips. Then she gets on her hands and knees in front of me, and takes my length into her small fingers.

Faster than lightning, her mouth is on me, and I can't help a primal groan. My tongue lolls out as she immediately brings me deep into her throat, her lips dancing along the underside of me. She makes all sorts of delightful slurping sounds as she pumps me with her hands, occasionally stopping to play with my furry balls.

"Are you going to put these to good use?" she asks, licking the fluid off the tip of my cock. I almost can't answer, I'm so hungry to be inside her.

"Yes," I try to say, but it comes out a ragged growl. "They're full and ready to put a cub in you."

"Good." She gives me a final suck, like one would clean off a popsicle stick, and retreats up the bed. I watch her curiously as she gets on her knees, then hooks her hands over the headboard so she's facing away from me, and her ass is up in the air.

Oh, fuck. I know what she wants.

I have to lick the drool off my fangs as I creep toward her, just remembering how I walked into that white-tiled room so long ago to find this in front of me, waiting for me. Her cunt is still so lovely, embellished with curly dark hairs that make me ravenous for her.

When I lick it, dragging my tongue through her creases, she grunts in displeasure. "Russ, please. Don't make me wait."

I arch an eyebrow, because usually she doesn't have a problem with me drinking her up before I fuck her. She writhes and cries and often gushes all over my muzzle.

"So, that's how much you want another cub with me?" I ask her, rising up onto my haunches behind her. I grab her ass with both hands, gently pressing my claws into her soft skin. "You want to get fat and round with me again? You want me to make you a mother a second time?" I guide my pink cock toward where she's waiting for me, slick in the silver light. Even her lovely pussy has changed since birthing my cub, and I can't wait to be inside it again.

"Yes," she moans. "Fuck all of it inside me. Please, Russ."

My eyes roll back in my head as I slip the tip between her soft, swollen folds. As always, I have to hold myself back from simply plunging into her and unleashing everything I have to give. I test her first, and she rocks back against me, trying to take more.

"Give me another baby," she moans, and I can't help it any longer. I thrust into her, and she cries out at my invasion. She's so wet for me that it's easy to slide back out, and then press in again, skating on a river of her eagerness.

But I don't give her my knot yet, not right away. I simply make love to her, languidly stroking in and out of her, seeking all the places that make her say my name like a prayer. When I find her favorite spot, I pick up my pace, targeting it relentlessly until she's trembling, her tight sheath clenching and spasming around me.

"Russ," she whimpers, her arms giving out underneath her. All I have to do is lick the scar of her mating bite, then she lets out a full-throated scream as she meets her pinnacle, and I almost lose my battle not to go off inside her.

But I've waited this long to find her, and I can be patient a little longer for my mate.

twenty-five

DEE

I ORGASM SO hard that my vision swims. I bury my face in the comforter, my muscles still twitching as I recover. But while I'm still sensitive, Russ starts moving inside me again, one slow inch at a time.

"Oh, fuck," I whimper, clenching and releasing as aftershocks ripple through me. But I'm softer now, and as he rocks in and out, even more of him starts to fill me up, bringing me home again. I have to grip the pillow hard as the twin swells of his knot push me open, spreading me wider for him one slow thrust at a time.

"Are you ready for it?" he murmurs, dropping down onto his forearms. I love the sensation of his fur gliding over my ass, his huge paws pinning down my hands.

"I'm so fucking ready."

Russ groans in satisfaction as he plunges in deeper, squeezing even more of himself into me with each stroke. It's easier to open for him now, since I had Ania, and he takes advantage of it as he pushes the rest of his knot inside.

"Oh, Dee," he moans, and this is the moment when commanding Russ becomes wild animal Russ. He yanks his cock out of me, then shoves that knot back in, triggering so many bursts of pleasure that my legs almost buckle. "I... I can't wait to..." He thrusts again, and noses the nape of my neck with his wet snout. "I can't wait to put another cub in you." Again and again he fucks his knot into me, and his drool dribbles down to my back so I know just how frantic I make him.

But I don't answer, because I can barely form words in my head. Just when I can't take any more, another inferno of a climax whirls through me, sweeping me up into the air. I sob Russ's name, and he lets out an animal snarl as he pumps his knot into me one final time. There, it sticks, and I bite my lip to keep from screaming as his incredible cock swells up even bigger, stretching me as far open as he can.

His hot come jettisons out, spreading an indescribable warmth deep inside me. I finally collapse to the bed, and he almost topples down on top of me as we both lie there, panting.

Russ hooks his snout over my shoulder and licks my ear, making me giggle. He gasps as I squeeze around him, and soon he's back up on his knees, pulling my hips into the air. With an obscene, wet sound, hot liquid rushes down the inside of my thigh.

"Can't waste any," he whispers to me, gathering it up in his paw and slathering it over where his knot already has my pussy spread wide. "I suppose I'll just have to fuck it all back into you."

And he does, over and over, until we're both sweating, gasping bodies, tangled up with one another. I lean back into him and his big arms wrap around me, clutching me close.

"I can't wait to see what comes out next," he whispers.

"You probably won't have to wait long," I answer, and he snorts against my hair.

By the time our wedding rolls around, I'm big and round again. It's Russ's second wedding, I know, but his cousins and brother assure me that they've never seen a wolfman quite as in love as he is with me.

Now that Russ can be there for the whole pregnancy, he's much more mellow, and lavishes attention on Ania and I both. He still doesn't like to be away from us, even when he has to go deliver babies, but I don't think that will ever change.

Trying to explain to my parents how we met was a bit of a mess, but they've quickly come around to the idea because they love being grandparents, even if some of Ania's wolfgirl antics don't quite make sense to them.

Boomer loves her, perhaps even more than he loves me.

As we stand in front of our assembled guests, I can't take my eyes off my handsome wolfman, even though I know the tight bowtie makes him uncomfortable. Before the officiant has finished talking, Russ grabs me around the waist and pulls me in for a wild kiss, and our audience goes crazy.

He holds me like that, promising me forever, with all the love in his body.

THANK YOU SO MUCH FOR READING!

If you enjoyed this book, please consider leaving a review!

Reviews are incredibly helpful to indie authors like me in reaching new readers.

You can also support me by buying my other books!

WHAT'S NEXT?

You can now get the next book in the DreamTogether Breeding Program series, *Bred by the Dragon*!

join my newsletter!

For all the latest regarding books, and to get access to a FREE novella, join my newsletter! You can also pick up signed paperback copies of your favorite books with art, stickers, and more!

www.LyonneRiley.com

also by lyonne riley

TROLLKIN LOVERS

ANTHOLOGIES

OTHER BOOKS

about the author

Lyonne Riley published her first book at age five, which was written on tiny sheets of notebook paper, and she insisted on giving a copy to everyone she knew. She's been writing ever since, from fan fiction in her teen years to original fiction as an adult. After a stint in traditional publishing, she discovered what she truly wanted to write: very smutty stories about monstrous beasts and the little humans they worship.

Now she lives in the middle of nowhere with her dogs and spouse, writing sexy fairy tales.

acknowledgments

I would like to thank everyone involved in helping me through the process of putting out this book. I can't say enough how much I appreciate the help and encouragement of the people around me—especially Amber, who told me I could do this in the first place.

Huge thank you to Rowan Woodcock for the gorgeous cover illustration. To my critique partners, who gave me phenomenal feedback: You all make this possible. And of course, my amazing spouse, who has always supported my dreams—and given me lots of inspiration for my characters' sexy adventures.

I couldn't have done this without the expertise of my fellow self-published romance authors. Thank you for inviting me into your circles and helping me through this process.

And thank you to my readers, who gave this book a shot.